CHERISH

What Reviewers Say About Kris Bryant's Work

EF5, *Novella in* **Stranded Hearts**

"In *EF5* there is destruction and chaos but I adored it because I can't resist anything with a tornado in it. They fascinate me, and the way Alyssa and Emerson work together, even though Alyssa has no obligation to do so, means they have a life changing experience that only strengthens the instant attraction they shared."—*LESBIreviewed*

Home

"*Home* is a very sweet second-chance romance that will make you smile. It is an angst-less joy, perfect for a bad day."—*Hsinju's Lit Log*

Scent

"Oh. Kris Bryant. Once again you've given us a beautiful comfort read to help us escape all that 2020 has thrown at us. This series featuring the senses has been a pleasure to read. ...I think what makes Bryant's books so readable is the way she builds the reader's interest in her mains before allowing them to interact. This is a sweet and happy sigh kind of read. Perfect for these chilly winter nights when you want to escape the world and step into a caramel infused world where HEAs really do come true."—*Late Night Lesbian Reads*

Lucky

"The characters—both main and secondary, including the furry ones—are wonderful (I loved coming across Piper and Shaylie from Falling), there's just the right amount of angst and the sexy scenes are really hot. It's Kris Bryant, you guys, no surprise there."—*Jude in the Stars*

"This book has everything you need for a sweet romance. The main characters are beautiful and easy to fall in love with, even with their little quirks and flaws. The settings (Vail and Denver, Colorado) are perfect for the story, and the romance itself is satisfying, with just enough angst to make the book interesting. …This is the perfect novel to read on a warm, lazy summer day, and I recommend it to all romance lovers."—*Rainbow Reflections*

Tinsel

"This story was the perfect length for this cute romance. What made this especially endearing were the relationships Jess has with her best friend, Mo, and her mother. You cannot go wrong by purchasing this cute little nugget. A really sweet romance with a cat playing cupid."—*Bookvark*

Against All Odds *(co-authored with Maggie Cummings and M. Ullrich)*

"*Against All Odds* by Kris Bryant, Maggie Cummings and M. Ullrich is an emotional and captivating story about being able to face a tragedy head on and move on with your life, learning to appreciate the simple things we take for granted and finding love where you least expect it."—*Lesbian Review*

"I started reading the book trying to dissect the writing and ended up forgetting all about the fact that three people were involved in writing it because the story just grabbed me by the ears and dragged me along for the ride. ...[A] really great romantic suspense that manages both parts of the equation perfectly. This is a book you won't be able to put down."—*C-Spot Reviews*

Temptation

"This book has a great first line. I was hooked from the start. There was so much to like about this story, though. The interactions. The tension. The jealousy. I liked how Cassie falls for Brooke's son before she ever falls for Brooke. I love a good forbidden love story."—*Bookvark*

"This book is an emotional roller coaster that you're going to get swept away in. Let it happen…just bring the tissues and the vino and enjoy the ride."—*Les Rêveur*

"You can always count on Bryant to write endearing and layered characters, even in stories like this one, when most of the angst comes from the not-so-simple act of falling in love."—*Jude in the Stars*

"People who have read Ms. Bryant's erotica novella *Shameless* under the pseudonym of Brit Ryder know that this author can write intimacy well. This is more a romance than erotica but the sex scenes are as varied and hot..."—*LezReviewBooks*

"This book is a bag of kettle corn—sweet, savory and you won't stop until you finish it in one binge-worthy sitting. *Temptation* is a fun, fluffy and ultimately satisfying lesbian romance that hits all the right notes."—*To Be Read Book Reviews*

Falling

"This is a story you don't want to pass on. A fabulous read that you will have a hard time putting down. Maybe don't read it as you board your plane though. This is an easy 5 stars!"—*Romantic Reader Blog*

"Bryant delivers a story that is equal parts touching, compassionate, and uplifting."—*Lesbian Review*

"This was a nice, romantic read. There is enough romantic tension to keep the plot moving, and I enjoyed the supporting characters' and their romance as much as the main plot."
—*Kissing Backwards*

Listen

"[A] sweet romance with a touch of angst and lots of music."
—*C-Spot Reviews*

"If you suffer from anxiety, know someone who suffers from anxiety, or want an insight to how it may impact on someone's daily life, I urge you to pick this book up. In fact, I urge all readers who enjoy a good lesbian romance to grab a copy."—*Love Bytes Reviews*

"If you're looking for a little bit of fluffy(ish), light romance in your life, give this one a listen. The characters' passion for music (and each other) is heartwarming, and I was rooting for them the entire book."—*Kissing Backwards*

"Ms. Bryant describes this soundscape with some exquisite metaphors, it's true what they say that music is everywhere. The whole book is beautifully written and makes the reader's heart to go out with people suffering from anxiety or any sort of mental health issue."—*Lez Review Books*

"I was absolutely captivated by this book from start to finish. The two leads were adorable and I really connected with them and rooted for them. ...This is one of the best books I've read recently—I cannot praise it enough!"—Melina Bickard, Librarian, Waterloo Library (UK)

"The main character's anxiety issues were well written and the romance is sweet and leaves you with a warm feeling at the end. Highly recommended reading."—Kat Adams, Bookseller (QBD Books, Australia)

Forget Me Not

"Told in the first person, from Grace's point of view, we are privy to Grace's inner musings and her vulnerabilities. …Bryant crafts clever wording to infuse Grace with a sharp-witted personality, which clearly covers her insecurities. …This story is filled with loving familial interactions, caring friends, romantic interludes and tantalizing sex scenes. The dialogue, both among the characters and within Grace's head, is refreshing, original, and sometimes comical. *Forget Me Not* is a fresh perspective on a romantic theme, and an entertaining read."—*Lambda Literary Review*

"[I]t just hits the right note all the way. …[A] very good read if you are looking for a sweet romance."—*Lez Review Books*

Shameless—*Writing as Brit Ryder*

"[Kris Bryant] has a way of giving insight into the other main protagonist by using a few clever techniques and involving the secondary characters to add back-stories and extra pieces of important information. The pace of the book was excellent, it was never rushed but I was never bored or waiting for a chapter to finish…this epilogue made my heart swell to the point I almost lunged off the sofa to do a happy dance."—*Les Rêveur*

Not Guilty—*Writing as Brit Ryder*

"Exquisite! I loved this story! I have heard so many good things about it and it did not disappoint as it was so much more than I expected. Kris Bryant, writing has her alter-ego was absolutely brilliant. The story is hot, passionate and filled with drama making a really exciting read. You can really feel the passion between Claire and Emery, that instant attraction between them was just perfect."—*LESBIreviewed*

"Kris Bryant, aka Brit Ryder, promised this story would be hot and she didn't lie! …I love that the author is Kris Bryant who, under that name, writes romance with a lot of emotions. As Brit Ryder, she lets chemistry take the lead and it's pretty amazing too."—*Jude in the Stars*

Whirlwind Romance

"Ms. Bryant's descriptions were written with such passion and colorful detail that you could feel the tension and the excitement along with the characters…"—*Inked Rainbow Reviews*

Taste

"*Taste* is a student/teacher romance set in a culinary school. If the premise makes you wonder whether this book will make you want to eat something tasty, the answer is: yes."—*Lesbian Review*

Jolt—*Lambda Literary Award Finalist*

"[*Jolt*] is a magnificent love story. Two women hurt by their previous lovers and each in their own way trying to make sense out of life and times. When they meet at a gay and lesbian friendly summer camp, they both feel as if lightening has struck. This is so beautifully involving, I have already reread it twice. Amazing!"—*Rainbow Book Reviews*

Touch

"The sexual chemistry in this book is off the hook. Kris Bryant writes my favorite sex scenes in lesbian romantic fiction." —*Les Rêveur*

Breakthrough

"Looking for a fun and funny light read with hella cute animal antics, and a smoking hot butch ranger? Look no further. ...In this well written, first-person narrative, Kris Bryant's characters are well developed, and their push/pull romance hits all the right beats, making it a delightful read just in time for beach reading."—*Writing While Distracted*

"[A]n exceptional book that has a few twists and turns that catch you out and make you wish the book would never end. I was captivated from the beginning and can't wait to see how Bryant will top this."—*Les Rêveur*

"*Breakthrough* delivers satisfying romance, amusing adventures, and a surprising, thrilling change of pace in the latter half of the story. Recommended for fans of 'fish out of water' stories, femme/butch pairings, Great Outdoors immersion, and the television series *Northern Exposure*."—*Omnivore Bibliosaur*

By the Author

Jolt

Whirlwind Romance

Just Say Yes

Taste

Forget-Me-Not

Shameless (writing as Brit Ryder)

Touch

Breakthrough

Against All Odds (written with M. Ullrich
and Maggie Cummings)

Listen

Falling

Tinsel

Temptation

Lucky

Home

Scent

Not Guilty (writing as Brit Ryder)

Always

Forever

EF5 (Stranded Hearts Novella Collection)

Serendipity

Catch

Cherish

CHERISH

by
Kris Bryant

2023

CHERISH

ISBN 13: 978-1-63679-567-6

THIS TRADE PAPERBACK ORIGINAL IS PUBLISHED BY
BOLD STROKES BOOKS, INC.
P.O. BOX 249
VALLEY FALLS, NY 12185

FIRST EDITION: SEPTEMBER 2023

CREDITS
EDITORS: ASHLEY TILLMAN AND CINDY CRESAP
PRODUCTION DESIGN: SUSAN RAMUNDO
COVER DESIGN BY DEB B

Acknowledgments

Grief is an ugly, powerful thing. I'm still adjusting to my mother's passing and it's not easy. Trying to be creative when your heart isn't in it is hard.

Thank you, Ash and Cindy, for being sensitive to my needs and giving me space to work at my own pace. Your guidance and kindness got me through the deadlines. Ruth was great at checking in to make sure I was doing okay (thanks for the pics of Remy), and I really needed the support. Thanks to Rad, Sandy, Toni, Stacia, and all the BSB crew for the extra effort. You all are amazing.

I wouldn't be here without my nuggets. I hid out in Chicago a few times with Rivs, and Jordan, and Clark, and Jordan Clark. I love them all. Ana and Morgs, my little sisters, are right there to lift me up and make every day we all spend together totally epic. I'll have these memories forever. Thank you so much for your love.

Our community on Patreon has grown into a group of friends. Thank you for your pledges and sticking with me. I still have so much fun and I appreciate your love and continued support.

I have so many friends to thank and not enough time or space to thank them all. I miss my bestie, Fiona, who is busy with life and raising even more ginger snaps, but one day our writing dates will pick back up. KB Draper and HS—your love and friendship will be with me forever. And Deb. You've been by my side during the worst time of my life and I so appreciate your love and understanding while I fumble through this great loss.

I love my readers. Everyone has been so kind. We have a small but loyal community and I'm honored to be a part of it. Thank you for reading my books and talking about them to the world.

Dedication

To my mom
I will love you and miss you forever

CHAPTER ONE

S he tried to get away. Her big, brown eyes darted back
and forth between the gate leading to the beach and me.
I could tell the toddler was calculating the distance, so I crouched
down ready to intervene if necessary. Her face scrunched up with
determination and she made it a few awkward steps until a very
attractive brunette grabbed her from behind and covered her face
with tiny kisses.

"Where do you think you're going?"

I smiled at the sweet exchange acutely aware that I, a total
stranger, was interrupting a personal moment on private property.

"Excuse me. Can you tell me if that's 819 Ocean View
Drive?" I pointed to the gray shingle beach bungalow with large
windows and a deck that wrapped around half the house. I had
looked the address up on Google Earth, but I couldn't find the
guest cottage that was supposed to be my address for the next
three months. Of course, it didn't matter where the cottage was.
After graduating from Rhode Island School of Design, this little
beach town would be a heavenly escape for the next several
months.

The woman twirled her finger in a circle indicating the
mansion she just exited, the bungalow I'd pointed at, a garage

off in the distance, and a shed almost the size of a house. "All of this is 819 Ocean View. Welcome to Revere Estates. You must be Josie. We've been expecting you. Hi, I'm Cassie Wellington." She reached out to shake my hand. "And this little escape artist is Ava."

"Hi. I'm happy to be here. Thank you so much for having me." My anxiety settled once I realized I was in the right place. For a brief moment, I thought I was trespassing and somebody was going to burst through the door, screaming at me to leave the property at once before they called the police. I was partially right. Somebody did burst through the door screaming, only it was an adorable toddler with light golden brown curly hair hell-bent on busting through the privacy gate that led to the beach. "So, I'm staying there?" I pointed to the large bungalow that I thought was the main house. Now I could see that it was dwarfed by the mansion on the other side of the driveway.

Cassie nodded and smiled. "Go ahead and park in the carport. If you need anything at all, just knock on the door or text us. I left our number on the counter inside your place." She was beautiful with a warm smile and brown hair that flowed down to the middle of her back. Her brown eyes, the same as Ava's, were welcoming.

"Thank you." Feeling rumpled from the trip, I smoothed down my wrinkled shirt and shorts and shook out the tingling from my long legs. My five-foot ten-inch frame was folded like a pretzel in my small Corolla for the last two hours. I wish I had time to make myself presentable before meeting my host family, especially now that I knew they were probably billionaires. I didn't have words to describe how fortunate I felt. I was twenty-three, a recent graduate, and had been given the opportunity of a lifetime, but looking at Cassie, who couldn't have been much older than me, and seeing how well put together she was made me realize how destitute I was. I had a long way to go before I was successful at anything, but I was hoping this summer would help put my art into the hands of people who could catapult my career.

"We're happy to have you." She slid a squirming Ava down her side until the toddler's sandals touched the cobblestone driveway. "Ava, this is Josie. Can you say hi?" Ava waved and ran over to the gate. Cassie looked at me. "Toddlers have two speeds. Super-fast and asleep." I smiled out of politeness. I knew nothing of babies or small children. I wasn't against them. I just hadn't spent any time with them. "Her mother and brother are down at the beach. She just woke up from a long nap. Would you like to join us?"

Immediately I shied away. "Oh, no thank you. I should unpack and get settled. It was a long drive." It wasn't, but I just arrived, and I didn't want to intrude.

She waved me off. "I get it. If you feel like exploring, you'll find us down there. Just make sure to always close that gate. Ava is a wanderer."

I nodded vigorously and filed that away under emergency advice in my head. The last thing I needed was Ava getting out and it being my fault. "Thanks again for everything. I'm so excited to be here."

"We hope you have fun this summer. Your artwork is amazing."

I hated repeating myself, so I nodded. "Thank you." I felt incredibly lucky when my portfolio was chosen for the Wellington residency. At the time, I didn't think about the logistics at all. Being here and seeing this gorgeous family and their gorgeous house made me feel way out of my league.

Cassie grabbed Ava's hand. "Okay, cuddle bug. Let's go see Mama." She looked back at me. "Maybe we'll see you down there."

I waited until they were out of the courtyard before I gaped at my surroundings. I parked my car under the carport per Cassie's instructions and let myself into the house. It had been described to me as an apartment but was really a three-bedroom house on the property that slightly resembled the main house. It was fully furnished and spacious.

The bedroom that faced the ocean was cleared out except for a large worktable with a note on it. *The lighting is excellent here and we figured this would be the room you want to create in.* Whoever wrote the note had smooth and steady handwriting.

The open kitchen was bright and full of updated appliances. On the counter there was a note in different handwriting with Cassie's phone number, the number for the main house, and instructions for parking and working the gate codes. Next to it was an envelope with my name written in calligraphy on the thick, heavy ivory paper. It was an invitation to the Wellingtons' kick-off-the-summer barbecue. Of course, I would go. It was going to be on the property so I didn't have to do much except walk out the door. Maybe I'd meet some really cool people this summer. I attached the card to the refrigerator with the only magnet I could find—a small red crab wearing a white tank top with Goda spelled out in pink letters. It didn't match the décor of the place but made me smile nonetheless.

I unloaded my car as quickly as possible. The back seat had rolls of canvas, wood, and the tools needed to stretch my own canvases, and the trunk had two easels, paints, pencils, brushes, and rags. That left the front seat for one small carry-on sized suitcase and two backpacks of clothes, shoes, and toiletries. If I had to do any socializing other than the Wellingtons' summer party, I might be in trouble. It didn't matter though. I was here to paint and hone my craft, not go to parties.

I had everything in the house in fifteen minutes. It was late afternoon and even though I still had hours before sunset, I didn't want to miss it. I wanted to explore, feed the hunger pangs that poked my stomach, and meet the rest of Cassie's family. I changed into a fresh T-shirt and shorts and grabbed my sandals. I had an exit door to the beach from the room that was going to be my art studio, so I never had to worry about the gate and accidentally leaving it open.

I didn't know what to expect when I met Cassie's wife and son. I thought Cassie was beautiful, but her wife literally took my breath away. Her pale blond hair was braided back away from her face. Their son, Noah, looked exactly like her. Both had light blue eyes and naturally red lips. I knew the family offering the residency was LGBTQ+ friendly, but I fell in love with them once I found out they were also members.

"Hi, Josie. We're glad you're here. I'm Cassie's wife, Brook, and that's our son, Noah. I heard you already met Ava," Brook said.

"She's adorable." I returned Ava's awkward wave. "You have such a lovely place in a beautiful part of the world. Thank you for inviting me to spend my summer here." I pressed my lips together to keep from over talking. It was a nervous habit.

"Do you want to help us?" Noah asked. He was sitting in the sand with Ava. They were building an impressive sandcastle out of molds that were far more extravagant than the plain plastic bucket and shovel I had when I was little.

"That's sweet of you to ask. Maybe next time. I want to take a quick walk and get to know the area." Honestly, I didn't want to interrupt. It was Sunday and I wasn't sure if they worked remotely and were headed back to their main residence somewhere else or were here full-time. Either way, I was sure they didn't want to spend their Sunday with a stranger no matter how nice they were.

"See you later," he said.

I casually strolled to the waterline anxious to feel the ocean on my feet and dig my toes in the sand. It was June and the water was still cold but refreshing. There was plenty of open space to set up and sketch or paint. Revere Estates must have been part of a private beach because I didn't see another person near the water.

I rounded a dune and, off in the distance, saw bright buildings that advertised kayaks and paddleboards. Several wooden decks extended far out from restaurants to give patrons the true ocean view eating experience. It was the quintessential quaint seaside town. Walking to it from Revere was probably faster than driving and trying to find parking in summer traffic. I made my way over to a public path and walked between an eclectic hardware store and quaint coffee shop. When I cleared the alley, I found myself in downtown Goda, Massachusetts.

It was a high-end town, but I was bound to find something cheap to eat. I hadn't eaten since breakfast and the restaurants smelled amazing. I'd saved up enough money this past spring at my on-campus job to have a little spending money for the summer and that included splurging on fresh seafood. I settled on a small casual restaurant with outdoor picnic tables that were bolted into something below the sand.

A balding older man, whose once white apron now had a splatter of yellowing grease stains across his massive chest, barked out from behind a window framed by a chalkboard menu. "What can I get you?"

"I'll have a lobster roll, chips, and a water."

He nodded and pointed his pen to the tables. "Have a seat and someone will bring it out to you."

I sat at a table closest to the beach and far away from the play area designated for children. It was beautiful here. The beach was clean with soft sand and very little foot traffic. I pulled out my phone and took several photos, but I knew they wouldn't do the view justice. One of my main goals was to paint landscapes and seascapes, and this was going to be the perfect place to do both.

A surfer-looking dude with bleach blond shaggy hair and a tan sneaked up behind me with my order. He put the plate down and dropped a pile of napkins in front of me. "Is there anything else?" he asked.

"No, thank you. This is great." I didn't realize how hungry I was until I took a bite. I wasn't expecting it to be so delicious and fresh. This would be my go-to when I didn't want to cook. I happily munched on my dinner and people-watched for the next half hour.

I googled the Wellingtons out of curiosity and my jaw dropped. Brook was CEO of Wellington Enterprises. I had no idea she was one of those Wellingtons. I was staying with one of the wealthiest families in the northeast. Their name wasn't on the grant when I accepted it so I never investigated further.

Still stunned, I discarded my trash in the appropriate bins and walked down the main street noting which shops I wanted to visit when they were open. There was so much money in this town. The cars were foreign, sleek, and expensive. The houses were massive and close together. I liked that Revere Estates was farther out and had more room than the domino houses in town. Goda had tons of art galleries that displayed several artists I had admired over the years. Tula Sims, O. Colburn, and Beckett Lemon were all on display. I'd only been in Goda a few hours and I could already tell this town would be my happy place. I walked back as the Wellingtons were gathering their belongings and automatically jumped in to help.

"Josie, would you like to have dinner with us tonight? We would love to get to know you better," Brook said.

"That would be great, thank you." Even though I ate an hour ago, I wasn't going to be rude and turn down a second invitation from them.

I carried a beach chair and two buckets of toys up to the house. Cassie opened the mud room to the main house and motioned me to enter. I couldn't wait to see the rest of the house later tonight.

"Why don't you come by in an hour?" Cassie asked after I handed her the toys. "Do you have any dietary restrictions?"

I shook my head. "None. Do you want me to bring anything?"

"Oh, no. You're our guest. We'll see you soon."

I took a quick shower and slipped into a summer dress. It was unfortunate that most of my wardrobe was boxed up and taking up space in my friend's basement. Art supplies seemed far more important than clothes when I packed. A decision I was now regretting after realizing that I was probably expected to socialize while I was here. My hair was just long enough to pull back into a stubby ponytail. Some pieces didn't quite make it and fell out, but I did the best I could.

With thirty minutes to spare, I headed back to the beach. I might not be able to watch the sunset my first night, but I could watch it drift into place. My heart swelled when the warm colors spread out on the sky's canvas as the sun dipped lower. It wasn't as impressive as a West Coast sunset, but it was still beautiful. I walked along the shore as waves lapped at my feet. I could do this every day and never get tired.

I turned and was startled by a woman who was sitting in the sand with her back against a small dune. Either I missed her on the way to the water, or she sneaked up behind me. My heart went from a slow and steady peaceful beat to hummingbird wings frantically pushing against my ribs in the span of two seconds.

"You scared me."

She lifted her eyebrow but didn't say anything.

I was in that awkward space of giving her all my attention and her not taking any of it. It was as if she was trying to look around me. "Oh. I'm sorry." I quickly moved out of the way but kept my eyes on her.

Her long brown hair was pulled back in a hair tie, but the wind had blown several pieces loose. Her dark eyes were focused on the ocean even though she had to have known I was staring. She was so beautiful, but there was a shadow of darkness in her features. Her full mouth dipped at the corners and her brows furrowed slightly on her forehead.

"Hi, I'm Josie," I said. When she looked at me, my heartbeat skipped. Why was I having such a reaction to this woman? It took all my willpower to keep from wiping my suddenly sweaty palms on my dress. "I'm staying with the Wellingtons."

"So, you're this year's artist-in-residence," she said. Her voice was low and raspy and her delivery cool. She made it sound like it wasn't a big thing or something that wasn't important. I wasn't deterred.

"Let me guess. You're the neighbor who dislikes outsiders," I said. Her gaze turned sharp and the corners of her mouth dipped more. She was almost frowning, but even that didn't take away from her beauty. The warm colors from the impending sunset cascaded over her giving her skin an ethereal glow. I was fascinated by her even though it was obvious I was not welcome in her space.

"Just the ones who stand in my view."

She continued to ignore me, so I quietly moved out of her line of vision and made my way back to Revere Estates.

CHAPTER TWO

I rinsed off my feet in the outdoor shower and quickly dried off inside. I brushed my hair and leaned closer to the mirror. My cheeks had pinkened from today's sun and from the awkward encounter with the lone woman on the beach. Who was she? Was she from here? Her linen pants, chic sleeveless blouse, and tasteful accessories told me that she had money. I assumed she lived in one of the large houses nearby. I pushed the encounter with her to the back of my mind and made my way to the Wellingtons' front door. I knocked twice and Noah immediately answered.

"Hi, Josie. Come on in." He was a polite, quiet kid.

I didn't have a lot of experience with children, but he struck me as somebody who was close to his family. I noticed how patient he was with Ava on the beach while they built that massive sandcastle. "Thanks, Noah. Did you have fun today?"

"Yes. I love it here," he said.

"Is the school year over?"

"Finally. We came up here for the summer a few days ago."

I followed him to a sitting room where Cassie and Brook were reading to Ava. Ava was fresh from the bath and wearing the cutest puppy pajamas.

"We're reading *Clifford, the Big Red Dog*," Cassie said. She whispered over Ava's head. "It's only a matter of time before we are guilted into rescuing a dog."

"Let's do it now. That way we'll have all summer to train it and play with it. I promise to feed it and walk it every day. It can even sleep in my room," Noah said.

I smiled at the dedication and promise in his voice. Hell, I was ready to find the nearest shelter because I whole-heartedly believed him.

"But then playing with your friends this summer would be cut short. Having a pet is a huge responsibility," Brook said. She gathered Ava and went around the room for everyone to say good night to her. It was so adorable watching this family.

"Sweet dreams, Ava," I said as they headed out of the room.

"Can I pour you a glass of wine, Josie?" Cassie asked.

"Yes, please." The view of the ocean was magnificent from the sitting room. I sank into the buttery-soft leather couch and accepted the glass from Cassie.

"Chef Patrick is grilling tonight and should be done soon," she said. I liked Cassie. Even though she had money, she seemed so down-to-earth and easy to talk to. Brook made me nervous now that I knew who she was. She seemed very intense.

"Oh, I'm fine. I mean, I ate a lot of junk food on the drive up here." Cassie sat across from me and even though I was wearing my best sundress, her casual outfit of shorts and a long-sleeved T-shirt and sandals made me feel drab. Her jewelry was plain, her makeup simple, but she carried herself so confidently that it was hard not to be impressed by her.

"Tell us more about yourself," she said. Noah sat in a chair and gave me his undivided attention as well. Why wasn't he in his room gaming or begging to ride his bike into town and grab ice cream with his friends? Maybe rich kids were expected to be polite and engaging. I didn't know anything about how the one percent lived or their guest rules.

"I'm twenty-three and I just graduated from art school. I love painting and mixed media."

"Which one is your favorite?" Noah asked.

"Painting is my default. I love oil on canvas, especially for landscapes."

"Is that all you do? Landscapes?" Noah asked. He seemed genuinely interested in what I had to say.

"It's my main focus. I tried everything in art school and always came back to that."

"The portfolio you submitted for the residency was gorgeous. I can't wait to see what you create here in Goda," Cassie said.

"Thank you. I can already tell I'll have plenty of material," I said. Her praise made me beam with pride. "My plan is to build up my portfolio as much as possible this summer. You can't do an exhibition or sell art if you don't have any completed paintings. Who knows? Maybe I'll even sell a piece or two."

"There are so many art galleries in town. Olivia, who lives two houses down, runs Monteclair Gallery on Ocean View Ave. I know she displays new artists all the time. I don't know if that's something you'd be interested in, but her gallery has amazing work," Cassie said.

I wondered if she was the woman I saw just a few minutes ago. "I might've met her just now. There was a woman on the beach staring out at the ocean." I didn't want to tell them about our awkward encounter because it was embarrassing so I kept it casual.

"What are we talking about?" Brook gracefully entered the room and sat next to Cassie. They held hands and I couldn't help but smile. They were such a striking couple.

"Josie was telling us a little bit about herself, and that she might have just met Olivia," Cassie said.

"Lone, quiet woman on the beach?" Brook asked. I nodded. "Yes, that's her." She waved her off. "Long story there. I do recommend her gallery though. She carries some artists with similar style to yours."

"I'll make sure to check it out," I said.

"Let's get back to you. You're a recent grad. Congratulations." Brook smiled and it was radiant.

"And she likes painting the most," Noah said.

"And she's very good at it," Brook said.

"Thank you." I felt a warm flush on my neck at her compliment. "I'm trying to add more to my portfolio and develop my craft this summer before I try to find something full-time." I feared food service was in my future. An artist getting a break right out of school was a long shot. Internships with huge artists was ideal, but very difficult to land. I was fortunate to have gotten this opportunity. I just needed to take full advantage of it.

"I think it's a great idea and I'm happy we could help. Now tell us what you like to do for fun." Cassie put her arm around Brook and scooted closer to be pressed up against her. Brook leaned into her. I almost melted.

"I like to watch movies, play games, hang out with my friends," I said. It felt like an interview. I wish I hadn't googled the Wellingtons. I went from chilling with them to sitting on the edge of the couch hoping everything I said was what they wanted to hear.

"Are you a gamer?" Cassie asked. Noah perked up when I nodded.

"I like *Elden Ring, Star Wars Lego, Fortnite...*" I was trying to list my "all ages" games in hope we would find something in common.

"You play *Fortnite*? I do, too!"

"We'll have to play sometime." I looked at Cassie and Brook for approval. They smiled at me. "Maybe on a day when the weather's not great. I brought my system with me."

"That would be cool. I'll save up my screen time," Noah said.

By the time we sat down to dinner, I was in love with this family. I wanted to know their story, but I didn't know how to ask it. By the end of the second glass of wine after dinner, I worked up enough nerve to ask. "How did you two meet?"

Cassie and Brook smiled at one another. Brook spoke first. "Cassie was Noah's nanny."

"Really?" My smile grew wider.

"Yes. I needed help and she needed a job. And then the magic happened."

"May I be excused?" Noah asked.

"You can have an hour of screen time and then it's bedtime. We have a big day tomorrow. We will be up later to say good night," Brook said.

"Why don't we head out to the deck? It's such a nice evening," Cassie suggested.

I grabbed my glass of water and followed them out. A staff of three immediately swooped in to clear off the table. I wondered how many staff members worked here. Did the children have a different nanny now? I was dying to know but didn't want to press. Thankfully, Cassie picked the conversation back up.

"Noah's tired of hearing the story, I'm sure. I was hired by Brook to take care of him when he was six. I needed a job after dropping out of med school, and Brook needed help. It took me a long time to knock down her walls, but I've never been happier." Cassie put her free hand on Brook's leg and softly kissed her cheek. The honeymoon wasn't over for them.

"How long have you been married?" I asked.

"We've been together six but married for five years. We had Ava two and a half years ago. She's a Christmas baby. The best present ever," Cassie said.

"I love your family so much already. Not that I'm looking, but I hope that one day I'll be as happy as you are."

Cassie laughed. "That's when it happens. When you aren't looking, and you least expect it. Mark my words, if it's meant to be, there's nothing you can do to stop it. And honestly, if it feels this good, why would you want to?"

❖

Painting on a beach was far more difficult than I romanticized in my head. I pictured myself standing in front of the water with my palette in one hand, a brush in the other, and the beautiful ocean nipping at my toes, but I forgot about windy days. The sand coated my wet canvas, my paints, and irritated my eyes. It was futile. I would have to wait until a calmer day. I brought my supplies back up to the estate and painted closer to the house. It afforded me some protection from the wind, but it wasn't ideal. I gave up for the day and decided to hit the galleries in town to check out the local art. I also wanted to find out if I met Olivia on the beach or if that woman was some random stranger.

I was careful not to smear my makeup when I slipped the sleeveless top over my freshly styled hair. The skirt was something I wore to art exhibits. It only hinted at sexy. I slipped on my flat sandals and decided to try my luck by driving into town. It was Tuesday and I hoped that summer traffic was only bad on the weekends.

"Have a great day, Josie." Noah waved to me from the gate. Cassie, Ava, and he were headed to the beach.

"Thanks, Noah. You, too." I carefully backed down the driveway and pulled onto Beach Front. The heart of Goda had parallel parking and I squeezed my fourteen-year-old car into a small space. Most of the galleries were houses converted into businesses. It was a blend that worked and wasn't overwhelming to the town. I grabbed my small messenger bag and slipped into Goda Gallery, the gallery located next door to Monteclair Gallery. I didn't want it to be obvious that my quest had something to do with trying to see Olivia again. The cool air whirled past me, and I quickly pulled the door shut.

"Hello." A friendly woman greeted me from a desk in the back of the small space.

"Hi."

"Is there anything I can help you with?" she asked. She was an attractive thirty-something with sassy black hair and blue eyes. She wore a black top and long flowy white skirt.

"I'm just looking around. Thank you."

"Let me know if you have any questions." She respectfully retreated to the back of the gallery where I was sure she was ready to pounce if I showed interest in anything.

I walked around the room examining each piece of art. Sculpture was fun, but there was something about a landscape painting that was so majestic. I didn't know how much time I lost standing in front of a Crowell oil painting, but I couldn't stop looking at it. It was an impressive three-foot by five-foot piece for the low price of twenty-two thousand dollars. I stared for several long, fascinating minutes. The boats at sea were getting tossed into the air as though the ocean was a cat batting them like toy mice. The details were so crisp and clear, and I loved every dark and stormy inch of it.

The woman came around the desk to look at the painting with me. "The artist lives in New Hampshire. His seascapes are very powerful," she said. She was humoring me. Or bored.

"One day, I'd love to paint something this grand." I paused to look at it again. "This bold and unpredictable." I pointed at the stormy scene and shook my head in awe.

"You're an artist?"

I nodded. "I just graduated art school." After seeing works like this, I knew I needed more practice. I was good, but this was amazing.

"Well, Crowell's been painting for decades. He's studied with some of the contemporary greats. I have a hard time keeping his work here for any length of time." There was pride in her voice. She probably thought I was just somebody coming in to get out of the sun but reconsidered once she realized I knew what I was talking about.

"It's a bit pricey for me, but I'm sure this will sell quickly. It's gorgeous."

She put her hands on her slender hips and nodded. "I already have a buyer interested, but I'd like for this to find a home here in town."

"I'm sure your gallery gets plenty of business from the locals," I said.

"We do. Tourists keep the other shops going, but art brings in a more specific crowd."

"Your window display drew me in. I noticed it this past weekend when I did a quick walk around town." I pointed at the series of marble sculptures arranged in the window.

"That's good to hear. I'm Beth, by the way." She held out her hand. I shook it.

"I'm Josie."

"Are you here for the summer or just a quick vacation to the cape?" she asked. My gaydar didn't ping so I figured she was just being friendly.

"I was awarded an artist-in-residence grant for the summer."

Beth looked impressed. "That's amazing. You were awarded a grant right out of school?" She had a great, welcoming smile and I found myself relaxing around her. She knew and appreciated art, she was friendly, and she was younger than most the people who lived here during the summer.

I gave her a brief educational history but didn't reveal where I was staying. The Wellingtons didn't put their name on the grant, so I figured they didn't want people to know. Chatting with Beth reminded me how much I missed my artist friends. It was hard to get close to people who didn't understand how draining creating art was. Most people thought it was a hobby. Our talent was getting gobbled up by computer-generated art. You could make a photograph look like a painting by downloading a simple program and a few clicks of a mouse. After half an hour with Beth, we were at the point where I was either going to have to buy something or leave. My bank account answered for me.

"Thanks for giving me a tour of the artwork on display. It's so nice to talk to people who appreciate art," I said.

"It's my pleasure. Come back any time," she said.

I walked out of the gallery and headed across the street for a coffee. I wanted to work up enough nerve to head next door to Monteclair Gallery and I didn't want Beth to see me head from her gallery straight to Olivia's.

"I'll have a vanilla latte, please." The overly chatty barista, Penelope, not Penny, was a college student working for spending money during the summer. Her parents owned the small bodega one street over. I stopped in it to pick up a few items when I first arrived in town and left immediately when I saw their prices. I would have to drive inland to find more affordable groceries and plan my meals. Six-dollar coffees weren't in the budget, but a girl needed her caffeine.

I thanked Penelope and casually strolled across the street to Monteclair Gallery, careful to avoid looking at Goda Gallery in case I made eye contact with Beth. I was playing the summer tourist to a T. Slow walk, coffee in hand, stopping to visit the local businesses. A sign on the door read *No outside food or drink allowed*. I downed the rest of my coffee and recycled the paper cup in a blue container by the stairs.

My eyes immediately found Olivia when I pushed open the door. As I'd hoped, she was the woman from the dunes. She was speaking with one of two patrons in the gallery. When she saw me, she paused in her conversation, but quickly redirected her attention to her customer. I took a deep breath and stepped to the left of the front door anxious to make my way over to her, but not be obvious about it. Within minutes, I was lost in a portrait by one of my favorite contemporary artists, O. Colburn.

"You've been standing in front of this painting for over five minutes." Her voice was low and smooth, and it took me a moment to snap out of my hypnotic trance.

I was surrounded by beauty. The painting in front of me and the woman beside me. I took a hard look at her before turning back at the painting, but my peripheral vision was working overtime. Long lashes framed an oval face with high cheekbones and full, plump lips. She stared intently at me. It was as though she was angry at me, but I had no idea why.

"This is incredible," I said.

She put her hand on her hip. "Oh? What's so special about it?" She smelled like fresh linen and was standing close enough that I could feel her body heat.

"Colburn isn't afraid of color. She uses purple when it should be green, and blue where it should be yellow. This art shouldn't make sense, but it does and the longer I stare at it and appreciate it, the more I want to cry." I blinked back a few tears.

How ridiculous was I getting so caught up in a painting? I came here to spy on the very person who I was tearing up in front of.

"You appreciate art then," she said. Her voice held a note of respect for me.

"I see something like this and it breaks me." I turned to her and smiled. "Do you personally know the artist?" She took a few steps back. Apparently, I was giving off intense vibes. I relaxed my shoulders and leaned my weight on one hip to appear chill.

"I do." That made sense since she was selling her art.

"How many pieces do you have of hers?" I glanced around the room to see if I recognized her style in other paintings around the gallery. I pointed to a smaller one of a tufted titmouse. "Oh, that's one."

Olivia looked impressed. "You really do know her style."

"Her portraits are phenomenal. And I love that her landscapes are more than beaches and stormy waters. Are you familiar with her series of old bicycles?" I asked.

"Yes, the Wheels series."

I turned to her. "I'm really sorry I ruined your quiet sunset the other night."

Her gaze traveled the length of my body and rested on my face. I knew she wasn't sizing me up but seemed to be seeing me for the first time. "You didn't ruin it. I'm Olivia Monteclair. Welcome to Goda."

I wanted to know why she brushed me off that evening because it was rude, but something warned me to tread lightly. "Thank you. So far, I love it here."

"Are you here for the whole summer?" She sounded robotic, like a cashier who asked if you were having a good day but didn't care either way.

"Until Labor Day. I hope to make the most of my time here."

She arched her eyebrow at me. "Congratulations on getting the residency. You must be very good."

I felt the heat rise from my stomach and brush the tips of my ears, my cheeks, and my neck. I knew I was good. "I'm not bad. Hopefully I'll create something like this some day." I waved my hand to include all the paintings in the gallery.

"I'm sure you will. Most of the artists here have decades of experience and you're just getting started," she said.

Even though I knew her words were true and Beth just said the very thing, I bristled and kept my ego in check. She had never seen my work. I'd been drawing charcoals and painting with oils for ten years. I took several private lessons and was near the top in my class at RISD. Every time I picked up a brush or pencil, I learned something new.

I forced my pursed lips into a smile. "You're right. My goal this summer is to hone my craft and learn as much as I can."

"I'm sure you'll do well. If you'll excuse me," she said and disappeared behind a wall to sit behind a desk with very little clutter.

No, I couldn't afford anything in this gallery, but her quickness at dismissing me irked me. Instead of feeling inspired like I did at Goda Gallery, I felt slighted. I left the gallery and visited a few more stores before I decided to head back to Revere Estates. Apparently, I had a lot more work to do since, according to Olivia, I had a lot to learn. It was one thing for me to know it, but a whole different game when somebody else pointed it out.

CHAPTER THREE

"W here are you going? Do you need a ride?" I asked. I was on my way to the hardware store for staples for my canvases. I remembered to pack everything but them.

"I'm signed up to take a drawing class at the college." Noah swung his leg over his bike and repositioned his backpack.

"That's cool. What kind of drawing class?"

He shrugged. "I don't know. Mom enrolled me last week." He pulled up something on his phone before handing it to me. It was a digital flyer from Goda's School of Art advertising *Still Life Drawing for All Ages*. "See?"

I quickly read it. It seemed like standard drawing class until I read the line at the bottom *Instruction by O. Colburn*. My mouth dropped. O. Colburn was the instructor! No fucking way.

"I definitely want to go to this. Why don't you let me drive you?" I asked.

"Let me ask Cassie if that's okay." While he raced inside to ask permission, I grabbed my charcoals and pastels and met him at my car. "Cassie said it was okay as long as you bring me home," he said.

"Not a problem at all. I think it's cool that you like art. Get in and buckle up." He threw his backpack in the back seat and strapped himself in. "What time does it start?" I asked.

"Nine a.m."

It was eight fifty. I looked at him and arched an eyebrow. "You were going to make it in ten minutes on your bicycle?"

"I'm pretty fast."

I didn't know if we were going to make it on time and we were in a car. "Well, let's get moving." No way was I going to speed. Worst-case, I could drop him off and circle for parking. I checked the clock. "The college is by the library, right?"

"Yeah. It's just past it," he said.

At least it was close. I turned the corner and pulled into the parking lot at exactly nine. We jogged into the building and followed the signs down the hall. Noah giggled when we both slipped on the freshly polished linoleum and banged against the vending machines. I rubbed my tender shoulder, knowing a bruise was forming.

"Ouch. Go, I'm fine. Go, go!" I waved him on. "Save yourself."

"Come on. We're not that late." He waited for me. What a sweet kid. He pointed to a room a few doors down. "It's right there."

The class hadn't started yet. There were about a dozen people in the room finding the perfect spot to draw. Noah was the youngest, but only by a few years. The oldest was easily in her sixties. To my surprise, Olivia was standing at the front of the class, waiting for everyone to settle in. The pieces of information quickly fell into place. Olivia was the O in O. Colburn. It explained why she had several art pieces in her own gallery. But why the secrecy?

I smoothed my stubby ponytail and looked down at my outfit. I instantly regretted throwing on the T-shirt with purple butterflies and my black jogging shorts. I had only wanted to meet O. Colburn, but this changed things. With as much dignity as I could muster, I marched over to her.

"Is it too late to join?"

She looked at me with a hint of annoyance at either the fact that I was here or that I was late. "This is a beginner's class."

Well, now she was irritating me. I smirked. "Are you saying I can't sign up for it?" I raised my voice a little so everyone in the class would hear. It was a dick move, but I was tired of her being dismissive of me.

She blew out a deep breath and sighed. "The class is two hundred and twenty-nine dollars. Grab a sketch pad from the stack and any pastels you'd like to work with."

I bit back my reaction knowing it was going to severely curb my goal of eating out a lot this summer. I held up my pencil case and small box of charcoals. "I only need the paper. Do you accept Venmo or Apple Pay?" I sent her the money and grabbed a large pad off the stack. It was the good kind of paper. Olivia didn't skimp on quality.

"Hello, class. My name is Olivia Monteclair and I run Monteclair Gallery on Ocean View. I paint under the name O. Colburn. Some of you might recognize my work. If you don't, that's okay. I won't fail you."

A slight woman in her sixties in the front of the class raised her hand. "Are you the same Colburn who painted that beautiful waterfront installation in Boston?"

"Yes, that's me." Olivia's curt answer made it appear that she didn't want to talk about her own work. "Any other questions about the class before we get started?"

I couldn't help myself. I raised my hand. Olivia stared at me and folded her arms in front of her. The motion was deliberately slow and I almost smiled.

"Yes?" she asked.

"Why Colburn?"

"It's my maiden name."

Of course, it was. I was an idiot for not knowing that. I'd briefly studied her in school and I wished I'd done a bit more research. But I was also angry that she didn't clarify at the gallery. Instead she let me fawn over her. I rolled my eyes. Whatever. She didn't owe me anything. She met my furrowed brow with an arched one and a tilt of her head.

"Please find a spot around the still life." As she spoke, she walked around the display set up in the center of the room. A bowl of oranges, apples, and pears was the centerpiece. Bunches of grapes were on one side of the bowl, and peaches on the other. Three flower vases sat behind the bowl. The display was gaudy, but it had items that were both easy and challenging to draw for a beginner. "Study one or two things that you find pleasing to the eye. You'll be working on it for a few days. I've set up artificial light that will be consistent throughout the morning. It's a good opportunity to work on shading and shadows."

Olivia waited until everyone was settled with their supplies before sitting by her sketch pad. The blank paper was already being projected onto the SMART Board. She did a quick demonstration of shading and let the class start. It was a beginner lesson, but she warned me before I paid.

From my desk at the back of the class, I could see the still life, but the assignment was to study one thing in the room. I didn't know why I did it. It was as if my hands were working on their own. I picked up a stick of fine charcoal and made a swoop across the page. I angled it and added thinner lines, focusing on the gentle curve of her lips. Where the lines were too heavy, I used my eraser to blot them. I switched my sticks as needed and by break time, I had a likeness to Olivia that I felt proud of. Though I was a bit mortified because I ignored the assignment and drew the instructor instead. I'd never felt such a strong need to draw somebody before.

"Can I see what you're working on?" Olivia asked.

I angled the pad toward my chest, hiding the image, careful not to smudge it. "Why didn't you tell me in the gallery who you were? I feel like an idiot for gushing about your art."

She shrugged. "It was refreshing to have somebody love my work without the prejudice of knowing me. I appreciated your honesty." She touched my arm, and it took everything for me not to react to her warm fingers on my skin.

The interaction was completely out of character for the woman I had painted in my head. The Olivia I knew was curt, opinionated, and borderline rude. Her reasoning made sense, but I still felt slighted.

"I get that. And I'd rather not show you what I've been working on until the end of class. I'm sure you understand." I was embarrassed that I deviated from the assignment. I was very pleased with it, but also mortified.

She held her hands up and took a step back. "I do." She looked at her watch. "Break is over in ten minutes. I recommend stretching and shaking your arms loose." She demonstrated it to Noah who came over to show me his drawing. He put his pad down on the table and shook out his arms. It was cute. "It feels good after having your arms up for an hour and a half." She smiled and worked her way around the room to the students who stayed in their seats during break, tweaking their drawings.

"Can I see yours?" Noah asked. He flipped his book open to show me a sketch of a bunch of grapes. It wasn't awful. His shading was off though.

"I'll show you mine when I'm done." I studied his drawing. "These are cool. I like how you drew the reflection of the light on the grapes."

He beamed with pride. It wasn't my job to correct him, but I was itching to tell him to blot the shading because it was too dark. Olivia was going to go around the room after break to have a one-on-one with each student.

I already decided that she wouldn't like mine—and not just because it was of her. Capturing the essence of someone was fucking hard. Anyone could draw a portrait with the right technique. Once you mastered the spacing, you could pretty much sketch anyone. But trying to get the curve of a cheek and the arch of an eyebrow to say what you wanted wasn't easy. I had sketched what I saw. A woman who was sexy, indifferent, inscrutable, with stunning eyes and full lips.

Drawing Olivia wasn't something I planned, but I wanted our break to be over so I could get back to it.

"Do you want anything to drink?" Noah pointed to the vending machines down the hall. Several classmates had coagulated around them as though they were the water coolers of corporate America.

"Yeah, let's get some sugar and caffeine and maybe be social." I checked myself. "Are you allowed to have sugar and stuff?" He nodded, but the smile perched on his lips was mischievous. I wasn't going to question him because it wasn't my place. "What are you getting?"

"Orange Fanta." He tapped a debit card against the card reader on the machine. "Since you drove and got us here on time, it's my treat."

"I'll take a Cherry Coke. Thanks, Noah. That's super sweet of you." We tapped our cans in cheers and talked about art for the rest of the break. Noah liked art because he said he saw different things than most people did. His goal was finding something unique about the simplest things. Those sounded like words of an artist. "What about photography? Have you tried that?"

"That class is in two weeks," he said.

I had a feeling he was going to love it. "Do you have a camera now?" I asked.

"I take a lot of photos with my iPhone. Did you know that some Hollywood directors have shot short films with just an iPhone? That's so amazing."

His excitement was palpable. The little dude was definitely going to love photography more. I was going to have to remember his schedule and check in with him. It made me happy to see a kid get super excited about art.

"Two more minutes," Olivia said.

We recycled our cans and headed back to class. My drawing pad sat undisturbed on the desk. I thought for sure she would peek, but nothing in her body language indicated she did. As we settled back into the assignment, I switched my charcoal to draw her long hair. Even though she had it braided back during class, I drew it down from the night on the beach. As I was finishing it up, it dawned on me at how utterly creepy it was to draw my instructor, so I quietly flipped a few pages and scrambled to find something in the still life to draw. I settled on a peach. It was boring, and with only thirty minutes left, she was going to be disappointed. I stuck with my charcoals and furiously sketched and smudged until class ended.

"You are more than welcome to leave your drawing pads here and I'll lock them up. Tomorrow we'll work on depth perception and tackle more of the still life," she said.

We both decided to leave the pads there. I wrote my name on the cover of mine and gave it to Noah. I made him in charge of handing them in and waited for him in the hallway.

"Are you ready?" I asked. He adjusted his backpack and nodded. I smiled at the small orange mustache that seemed even brighter against his pale skin. "Is there anywhere you want to go since we're in town?" I knew I was responsible for getting him home, but if he had things to do, we might as well knock them out now.

"Can we swing by the library?" This kid was my dream kid. He loved art and books.

"Sure. We passed it on the way here, right?"

"Yeah, it's down this way." He pointed down Beach Street. "Near the pizza place."

"Have you spent every summer here?" I asked.

He nodded. "My whole life."

"You must know everyone in town. Are there a lot of kids here?"

"I have a few friends that stay the summer here. They aren't here yet. Hayden won't get here until July fourth and Owen gets in next week," he said.

"Do you go to school with them?"

"Hayden and I go to Hessick Academy. Owen goes to a different school, but we're in the same grade."

"Are you all gamers? Are you carrying your system with you? Is that why your bag is so heavy?" I lifted a corner and felt bad when I let go of it and Noah stumbled.

"I have books I'm returning. I also have sunscreen, swimming trunks, and aqua shoes because you never know when you're going to want to jump into the ocean," he said.

"You just got here, and you already have books to return? Good for you," I said. He made a very good point about the importance of having swimwear within grasp. I made a mental note to keep board shorts and a bikini top in my car for that scenario.

"I have three books about sharks. There are at least ten species that live around Cape Cod. You can even swim safely with some of them. How amazing is that?"

"Yeah, no thanks. I don't want to have an encounter with one. I'll stay close to shore." I held the door open for him and followed him to the front desk. The woman behind the desk lit up when she saw Noah.

"You're back already? That was fast." She scanned the books and put them on a cart behind her. "What are you going to read about this week?"

"This week I'm reading *The Golden Compass*. We already have the book at home. I'll be back next week when I get to pick. Maybe I'll pick up books on whales."

"I'll look for your request online." She winked at him and waved when we turned to leave. She paid me zero attention. Not that I wanted any, but a hello would've been polite.

"Thanks for driving, Josie," Noah said when we pulled into the driveway. Cassie met us as I pulled up in front of their door.

I leaned over in the passenger seat after Noah vacated it to tell Cassie my impromptu plans. "I hope it was okay that I offered to drive. I signed up for the class, too."

Cassie waved me off. "It's fine. He was running a little bit late today." She turned her attention to Noah. "Did you have fun? Learn a bunch of stuff?"

"I drew grapes. Josie liked them."

"What did Olivia think?" Cassie took his backpack and walked with him to the house. She waved. "Thanks again, Josie."

Apparently, the entire world knew Colburn was Olivia except for me. I pulled into my spot. The sun was beginning to sting my skin and my stomach rumbled from lack of food. I grabbed a banana and a jar of peanut butter and pulled out my sketchbook. Today was inspirational because even though I felt duped, I got a lesson from one of my favorite artists. I promised myself that tomorrow would be a learning day and not a try-to-impress-a-woman day. I was here in Goda to fine tune my art, not get sidetracked by a crush.

CHAPTER FOUR

W hat about today? Do I get to see your drawing?"
Olivia asked.

I looked up from the sketch pad to find her standing in front of me. I pushed the pad away from me so she could get a better look. Today, I didn't have anything to hide. Grapes, pears, two peaches, and a rose in a bud vase. Very simple, boring, but good exercise.

Her eyes traveled the page. She pursed her lips and studied it a bit harder than I expected. Her hair was loose around her shoulders. It made her seem more approachable than when she wore it back.

I leaned back in my chair and crossed my arms, forgetting that my fingertips had a fine dusting of charcoal. I was careful not to wipe my hands on my jeans or my royal blue top. I'd dressed like an adult today and not like a teenager who threw on whatever was kind of clean. At least my shirt wasn't white like hers. She wore a sleeveless top with navy high-waisted, wide-legged pants and strappy sandals with a small heel. It was hard not to stare at her and since she was holding my sketchpad, I had the opportunity to look at her without it being awkward.

"Josie, right?" Wow. Okay, that was a bit rude. I nodded. "Why are you taking my class?" I shrugged. I did it to spite her because her coolness toward me was unwarranted, but then I saw it as an opportunity to learn from someone I considered to be great.

"Noah said he was going to a drawing class, and I was intrigued."

She nodded slowly but didn't look at me. She was focused on my sketch. After a few long seconds, she slid the pad over to me. In a clipped voice, she said, "You're good. You don't need to be here."

"I paid to be here."

"I don't know if I can teach you anything new. At least not in a beginner drawing class. You obviously know everything I'm teaching," she said. Her voice had dropped lower. The rasp of it gave me a chill.

"I'm sure you can teach me something." My eyebrow lifted at the innuendo and I felt the swipe of a blush on my cheeks.

For the first time all morning, she looked at me. She wasn't angry. She was hurt. Something had hurt her deeply.

I sat up straighter when I realized her frostiness was a defense mechanism. "And this is good practice for me. It's important to remember the basics. Plus, I'm Noah's ride."

"As long as you're okay with simple lessons," she said.

I pushed all kidding aside. "I appreciate any help."

She nodded and moved on to the next student.

I quietly flipped to her hidden portrait and shaded her eyes more and drew in a small mole on her jaw. She was beautiful. And sad. That's what was missing. I tweaked a few features, used my kneaded eraser on others, and smudged her jawline to soften it. I was honestly impressed with how it was turning out. Whenever we'd drawn live figures in class, I couldn't connect with the models. The result was always a technically perfect portrait with no real emotion. This drawing felt alive.

"That's Miss Olivia," Noah said.

I looked up in time to see his eyes widened with surprise. Shit. Nobody was supposed to see it. "It is, but I'm not finished. Are you done with the assignment?"

He pointed to the nearly empty room. "Everyone is. We're the only ones left. Has Miss Olivia seen this?"

I shook my head and lowered my voice. "No, and I don't want her to until it's done. I'll show it to her later. Are you ready to go?"

"Yeah, I'll turn in our pads."

"I'll start the car." Today was the hottest day so far on the cape. It was in the low eighties with very little breeze. I wanted to get the air going even though it was only a ten-minute drive home.

Noah left the building and crossed the parking lot to my car. His stride carried such confidence, but his face was still so innocent. He slid into the front seat and buckled in.

My sudden desire to work on portraiture was surprising to me. After spending two days sketching Olivia's portrait, I wanted to see if I felt comfortable doing somebody else and Noah seemed like the perfect candidate.

"Listen. I have an idea. What do you think about me painting your portrait as a gift to your moms? Would you be cool with that?" I asked.

"Sure." He smiled and looked at his reflection in the cracked sun visor mirror. He brushed his bangs away from his eyes and rubbed the charcoal smudge off his cheek. "Would I need to pose or something?"

"Yeah, if you wouldn't mind. I'll need you to stand still while I sketch. We can do it in the studio at the house."

"Sounds fun. When? Now?"

"Yeah, if you have time. When do you have golf lessons?" I knew the Wellingtons went to the country club on Tuesday afternoons. Noah said they swam with Ava while he did nine holes with a professional instructor.

"At four, but I need to eat first," he said. The traffic was thickening up because it was lunch hour, but we still made it home quicker than if he had ridden his bike. It was only noon so we would have plenty of time. "Thanks for the ride, Josie. What time do you want me over?"

"Whenever you're done. I'll just be in the studio so you can come in that back door if you want. And don't say anything since this is supposed to be a surprise. Tell them you're helping me with an art project."

"Okay. Do I need to change my clothes?" He looked down at his light blue polo and white shorts and topsider shoes. The kid looked like money. The shirt made his pale blue eyes pop more than usual.

"No, what you're wearing is great. See you in a bit."

He smiled and ran inside his house. I punched in the combo to mine and headed to the kitchen. I knew that I would forget everything like eating when I started a new project, so I made a quick sandwich from the last two pieces of bread. The Wellingtons had stocked the guest house with things like soup, crackers, healthy chips, and all types of nut butters. After paying the fee for Olivia's class, I was going to have to take them up on their generous pantry.

I set up the easel and decided on a sixteen-by-twenty-inch canvas. When Noah knocked on my door, I had the studio set up.

"So, first I'm going to sketch you, then I'm going to paint you. Does that sound good?" I asked.

"Sure. You want me to sit here?" He pointed to the stool I'd set up for him.

"Yes, if that's comfortable," I said. He sat and I almost died at the beautiful light that shone through the window and rested softly on his face.

"I'll try not to move." He was very serious. "Should I smile?" he asked through clenched teeth.

"I'm sure your moms would love it if you did, but I'll paint you however you want me to. This doesn't need to be serious."

"Okay. I'll smile. Is this okay?" He smiled softly. His light blue eyes also held a hint of laughter along with innocence and beauty and truth.

"That's perfect. Do you mind if I take a few photos? Then you won't have to sit so long."

He nodded. I snapped a few photos, then started sketching. I drew his basic proportions, making sure his eyes and nose were spaced correctly. Once that was done, I focused on his facial features. After forty-five minutes, I told him he was free to go.

"Josie, you're good. That really looks like me," he said. The excitement in his voice was hard to miss and I was afraid he would ruin the surprise.

"Thanks for being such a good sport about this. And don't tell your moms. I would like for it to be a surprise," I said.

"I won't say anything."

I knew he was being sincere, but twelve-year-olds weren't exactly known for their discretion. Time was of the essence. I had to finish this before he accidentally let it slip. Luckily, I was very focused once I started a project. I spent the rest of my afternoon glued to the canvas. It was almost eight in the evening by the time I stopped for the night. I was very happy with what I had created so far. I carefully wrapped my supplies and scrubbed the paint from under my nails. I was less than halfway done with his portrait, but my back and neck were stiff, and I needed a break and food. I grabbed a water bottle and a bag of chips and headed out to the ocean to sit and watch the waves. Was this what my summer was going to be like? Days of intense creating, poor eating habits, and exhaustion? I needed to curb my college habits and act like I didn't have deadlines because I didn't. This was supposed to be a growing experience.

"I hope that's not your dinner."

I froze, a chip halfway to my mouth, and turned. Olivia was tucked in the tiny dune like before, hidden from anyone on the beach.

"Why must you always scare me?" I asked.

She arched her brow. "I was here first. Both times."

I looked down at the bottle of wine and small container of figs, goat cheese, and grapes. "Is that your dinner?" It was meant to tease, but her food looked yummy.

"It's something."

I held up the bag of chips. "I'd share but there are only crumbs left."

"I'm good with what I have," she said. Her long hair was gathered over her left shoulder. She was wearing white pants rolled up to mid-calf and a peach-colored top with cap sleeves. A beach towel was draped over her shoulders for added warmth. Her painted toes were half under the sand, and it made me smile to see someone I thought was so uptight loosen up with such a small, carefree gesture.

"Class was fun today," I said.

When she looked up at me, my stomach dropped. The sadness on her features was unmistakable. She was in pain. I relaxed my stance so I didn't seem so confrontational.

"I still think you're way too good for it. I can't possibly teach you anything new." She sounded like a broken record. She didn't realize that her teaching the class was the draw.

"I doubt that. Like I said in class, practice. It's all about practice," I said. The wind picked up and she covered her wine glass with her hand. "I've accepted that all of my beverages, clothing, shoes, and art supplies are going to be covered with sand for the next two and a half months." She was quiet. I shrugged. "Beach problems, am I right?"

"It's a good problem to have." She pointed at my shorts and T-shirt. "Even though that looks good—I mean comfortable. You might want to bring a sweater. It gets chilly by the water when the sun goes down and the wind picks up." Olivia just complimented me. I picked up the hesitation when she corrected herself, but she said "looks good" and I was going to ride that for as long as I could.

"I'll remember that for tomorrow." It was my way of telling her I would be here every day, but since she wasn't inviting me to sit, I continued my walk down to the water. "Have a nice night, Olivia."

I didn't hear if she said anything. I walked in the soft sand where the ocean washed over the beach. I found a few colorful shells, most of them broken, but washed them in the water and slipped them into my pocket. I kicked the seaweed out of my way and walked until the sun sank lower on the horizon. I turned and easily found Revere Estates off in the distance. It was impressive even this far away. Cassie and Brook had their lights on outside and along the walkway up to their place. I wondered if Olivia was still hiding in the dune or if she went in because it was getting dark. I turned on the flashlight on my phone and made my way back to the welcoming lights.

"You should probably bring a real flashlight on nights you wander off." Olivia's voice was clipped again as though she was angry with me. What was with her? Why did she have a problem with me? I was ready to snap back at her, but as my instructor and Brook and Cassie's neighbor, I owed her the courtesy of not unloading on her.

"Again, with the scaring. Do you lurk in the shadows on purpose? Because that makes three times now." I held up my fingers as though my words weren't getting though. "Three times."

She stood and brushed the sand from the back of her legs. "I was worried."

I pointed to my chest. "For me? Why? This is the safest place on Earth."

She quickly grabbed her wine bottle and box of treats. "Never mind. You're right. You're not my business."

She was even graceful stomping off on the sand. I didn't know how I managed to get under her skin so quickly, but I was going to avoid her from now on. I sighed, realizing I had flushed over two hundred dollars to impress a woman and the only thing I got out of it was icy content. I wasn't going back. I shot off a text.

Hey, Noah. You'll have to ride your bike to class tomorrow. I'll be late.

He responded within a few minutes. *That's okay. Cassie said she'd take me. I'll see you there.*

Bye! I tried to sound excited even though I wasn't. Every day was a learning experience, and I was sad that my stubbornness would keep me from studying with one of the contemporary artists I admired most. I decided I would work on Noah's painting tomorrow instead. It would take at least one day to dry to the touch and weeks to completely dry. Maybe I could finish it by this weekend.

I was grumpy when I finally got to my place. What did I ever do to her? Why was Olivia such a snob? Did everyone in Goda think they were better than everybody else? Except for the Wellingtons and Beth at Goda Gallery, everyone else had given me the cold shoulder. I locked up and crawled into bed. Tomorrow was a new day. I tried to focus on colors I was going to use for Noah's hair but fell asleep with visions of a beautiful woman with long, chestnut brown hair, full curved lips, and sadness in her eyes.

CHAPTER FIVE

*A*re *you coming? Miss Olivia asked about you.*
I snorted when I saw Noah's message. Why did she care? She got her money. *I'm in the zone on your painting and can't stop.* He didn't need to know about our weirdly passive aggressive relationship.

OK. At least he responded.

I'll see you later. Learn all the things today.

He sent me a thumbs up emoji.

I kept working until I looked out and saw how calm the beach and ocean were. This was the perfect time to be outside and painting. I quickly grabbed my supplies and raced down to the beach. I planned on painting the dunes and the houses nestled in the sand, but I found a bright orange starfish on some rocks instead. It was surrounded by wet sand that glistened in the warm sun. Seaweed and shells dotted the perimeter. I was desperately trying to capture everything I saw but couldn't help focusing on the little details. I snapped a few photos to reference later.

"It's a good idea to take a break in this heat." Cassie stood behind me with a bottle of water, a tube of sunscreen, and a hat. "I know that it's hard to stop when you're creating, but I don't want you to pass out."

I licked my lips and squinted as though seeing my environment for the first time. "Thank you so much. Now that you mention it, it's hot out here." I downed half the bottle in front of her and plopped the floppy hat on my head.

"I came down here to remind you that our cookout is this weekend. We left the invite on your counter. It's low-key. Like a kickoff to summer." She pointed behind her. "The crew is setting up the stage and dance floor now." That was not low-key. They probably invited the whole town.

"Sure. Can I bring anything?"

She waved me off. "Oh, no. It's our treat. Just a chance for people to relax, eat good food, and get to know one another. And there will be plenty of art aficionados looking to make connections. We can introduce you around."

I blushed. "Thank you. Sounds like fun." I knew this residency would give me time to paint, but it never occurred to me how many connections it would open up.

"Don't stay out here too long. Sunburns are awful."

I quickly applied the cream to my hot arms and face. "You're my savior. Thank you."

I spent another hour on the beach until my light shifted. The starfish was long gone. I checked the time. It was two thirty. I'd forgotten to eat today, and my stomach growled with a reminder. I packed up my supplies and hauled everything back to my studio.

I grabbed a bag of apple chips and took a cool shower. My shoulders and face were sunburned. While it felt good to get some much-needed vitamin D, I was regretting the length of time I stood on the beach. I slipped on a loose T-shirt and a pair of boxers and turned my attention to Noah's portrait. Coming back to it inspired me. It was good. Like really good. I had a good idea of who Noah was and couldn't help but think that was why I was able to capture him so well.

I worked on his white-blond hair, adding bold colors like purple and blues. I gave the background a smoky tint and worked very hard on his small smile and bright blue eyes. I wrapped my brushes at ten. I was exhausted and sore from sitting still, and my sunburn hurt. I needed to move to get the blood circulating again so I opted for another late-night walk on the beach.

I carefully slipped on a sweatshirt and grabbed a flashlight. The moon was bright and reflected off the water. I almost didn't need the flashlight, but Olivia's words from last night echoed so I shone it in front of me to avoid pokey things like sticks, broken shells, and rocks. It was beautiful here. I was never going to be rich enough to live in Goda or any beach town, but I liked to pretend, and tonight I was a famous painter. People from all over the world begged me to paint them something, anything, just to have something with my name on the lower righthand corner.

"We missed you in class today." The voice was so quiet that I almost thought the soft noise was coming from the waves that lazily rolled onto the beach. Once again, I was startled but not surprised. Olivia was always out here.

"I got wrapped up in a project. Plus, you said I didn't need the help," I said.

The way she stared at me in the moonlight was unsettling. And why was I being such a bonehead? Maybe she didn't think I could see the hurt in her eyes, but it made me want to gently pull her into a hug. My guard was instantly down.

"Do you feel like going for a walk?" I pointed in the opposite direction of town.

"Sure."

Her response was surprising, but I was relieved that she hadn't shut me out again. I started the conversation with something innocuous that neither one of us could interpret the wrong way.

"What's your favorite thing about Goda?" I shone the flashlight a few feet in front of us careful to keep the beam steady while we walked down to the waterline. The sand was firm under my feet and gave me better traction. "Because my list is long." She made a small, pleasant noise that resembled a soft laugh. I wanted to hear it again because it was normal, and I could almost feel the tension between us drifting away.

"I like the peace out here by myself. And small-town life is less than a mile down the road. I know most of the businesses and the people. Plus, there's trust here."

"What do you mean trust?" I lived in a big city compared to Goda. I didn't even trust my neighbor to feed his cat. I didn't trust my roommate to not eat my food that was clearly marked in the refrigerator and on the pantry as mine. Trust wasn't something I embraced.

"I can leave my doors unlocked at the house and leave my keys in the car without worrying that somebody will drive off. I can't do that in Boston," she said.

"This is a pretty posh town. I mean, if I was a criminal, I'd make a killing out here," I joked.

"Everybody sees everything. That's also one of the downfalls of small-town life. Your business is everyone's business. I'm sure half the people knew who you were before you even arrived."

"But the Wellingtons are so private." It made sense on why they didn't put their name on the grant. Maybe the wrong people would apply for the wrong reasons. Money made people do weird things.

"They are, but this is their fourth year offering up a residence for either half the summer or the full summer. The locals are always curious." Olivia stepped on something sharp and leaned her body against mine. Instinctively, I put my arm around her waist and steadied her. The slight curve of her breast pressed into my ribs and I held my breath. For a brief moment, I felt her relax against me before the tension returned and she pulled out of my embrace. "I'm so sorry. I didn't mean to fall into you."

"I mean, I'm used to women falling at my feet, but never in my arms." The joke was slightly inappropriate, but I wanted to make light of what just happened. Olivia struck me as the kind of woman who only asked for help when necessary. She was probably fighting embarrassment and I wanted to let her know that it wasn't a big deal. Just because my heart was racing and my skin still tingled when her arm touched mine didn't mean that it was anything other than a stumble.

"I believe you. I mean, tall, attractive artist staying with one of the most prominent families on the East Coast? Of course, women are going to throw themselves at you."

"Because of the tall, attractive artist part or the wealthy family blah blah part?" I shined the light so I could see her face, but not blind her in the process. There was a slight smile perched on her lips. "Wait, is that a smug look on your face?"

The corners of her mouth flattened and she shook her head. Olivia Monteclair was playing with me. Frozen ice queen, borderline bitchy art instructor, was teasing me. A tickle of a new emotion rose from my stomach and landed somewhere in my chest. I wasn't prepared for the foreign feeling, and I put my hand on my stomach to settle it.

"Are you okay?" she asked.

I wasn't about to tell her being out here on the beach at night was doing funny things to my body. I didn't want to give her that kind of power. I downplayed it. "Oh, I'm fine. I just ate too many potato chips." I sucked in a breath and held it when I felt her fingers on my arm again.

"Hey, we can go back."

I waved her remark off. "I'm fine. I just had a bad day eating the wrong food."

"Like chips?"

I nodded. "Like chips. I will say that the Wellingtons have stocked the shelves with healthy food, but sadly, I veered off course and bought a bag of the greasy kettle fried ones." I liked that our conversation was light and yesterday's tension was forgotten. I picked up a broken sand dollar that was barely poking out of the wet sand. "What's been the biggest find on this beach? Have you found any treasures? Cool sea glass or conch shells? I saw a starfish earlier today, but it slid back into the ocean. I got several photos of it though." I told myself to stop talking and give her time to add to the conversation.

"I don't think anything important has washed up on this beach in years."

"Then what about coolness factor? Like my orange starfish." There was enough moonlight reflecting off the water that the flashlight wasn't necessary. She dipped her toe into the soft foam that gathered at our feet. She stopped to pick up a piece of sea glass and held it up to the moon. I shined the flashlight on it. "That's beautiful."

"We don't get a lot of large sea glass on this beach, and I rarely find them at night," she said. She slipped the piece into her pocket and continued to look around for more.

I found a broken clam shell and used the sharp edge to draw in the wet sand away from the tide. I drew a shark with its mouth open, showing two rows of sharp teeth. When Olivia's shadow loomed over me, I leaned back to show her what I'd been working on. My hand brushed her leg, and I pulled back quickly as though her warm skin scorched me. I played it off as though I hated the feeling of the wet sand on my hand, because I didn't like how my body was reacting to her nearness.

"Oh, that's great. Hopefully it's far enough away from the water that the tide won't wash it away before somebody gets to see this." She placed one of her shells in the middle of its mouth and sketched out a few lines to make it look like a fish.

"You just made it better."

She beamed at me. In that moment, she was perfect. Her sadness was replaced with a lightness I hadn't seen on her before. It must've shown on my face because she cleared her throat and took a few steps back. The magical moment was gone. I tossed the broken shell back into the sea and casually walked back to the water hoping she would follow and we could continue our late-night stroll. We walked in silence for a few minutes before the quiet was killing me.

"You said you have a place in Boston? Where is it?" I skipped a flat, smooth rock over the water and watched it bounce four times before slipping underneath the surface.

"I have an apartment in Beacon Hill."

I lifted my eyebrow and nodded. "That's a pretty nice area." Those apartments and houses were several million dollars. An apartment in the big city and a gorgeous house on the beach had to cost a fortune. She made money from her art, but I couldn't imagine it was enough to pay for everything. "You have such a lovely home, but you're always out on the beach." I didn't think she heard me because she didn't say anything. I was about to change the subject to something really offensive like the weather, but my ears picked up her low voice.

"I lost my husband and daughter to the ocean, and being on the beach makes me feel close to them."

Of all the things she could drop on me, that one I felt in my heart and my gut. It made me feel weak. I stopped and stared at her. "Oh, my God. I'm so sorry." There was nothing else I could or would say. It wasn't polite to gape at her or ask her what happened even though every part of my being wanted to know.

"I'm sorry. I know I shouldn't just blurt something like that out." She touched my arm, and the contact of her fingers against my sunburn stung. I held my breath at the momentary fire I felt through my thin sweatshirt. "I suppose I assumed you already knew."

"I didn't. But if you need or want to talk about it, I'm here."

"I'm surprised no one told you. Most people can't wait to tell newcomers about the great tragedy that struck Goda." There was bitterness in her voice.

"No. Nobody has said a word to me. But truthfully, I haven't really talked to anyone in town other than the Wellingtons. I pretty much keep to myself."

Her chest rose and fell as she took several deep breaths. "My husband, Andrew, and our five-year-old, Miranda, were flying to Nantucket in our plane. He thought they could beat the storm and circled out to sea to avoid the brunt of it, but…" her voice trailed off. Her hands curled into fists. "I told him not to go. I should've pushed harder."

"How long ago? If you don't mind me asking." I hadn't had any experience talking to somebody about this level of grief. I didn't know if I was being nosy or if I was helping.

"Three years." She wiped an errant tear from her cheek. I pretended not to notice. We kept walking.

"How long were you married?"

"Eight years," she said.

"I'm so sorry, Olivia."

She nodded and seemed to understand that there wasn't anything I could say. "It's late. We should probably head back," she said.

We turned around. I was hoping for the night to end better than it started, but her devastating news splashed over me like a strong wave. We walked most of the way back in silence.

"If you ever need to talk, I'm here. I'm a great listener," I said.

"Thank you, Josie. I appreciate that. I'll see you in class in the morning."

I cringed. "I'm sorry. I won't be there. I'm trying to finish something I'm working on for Brook and Cassie."

"But you paid a lot of money to take the class."

I nodded and thought, boy did I ever, but shrugged as though the money wasn't important. "You know how it is. Inspiration strikes when you least expect it. Plus, I'm afraid that since Noah knows about it, he might accidentally spill the beans and tell Brook and Cassie. It's supposed to be a surprise. A thank you for giving me the residency."

She gave a short laugh. "I completely understand."

"It's ridiculous, I know."

"I'll send your sketchpad home with Noah." Fuck. I hope she hadn't flipped through the pages. The look on her face told me she hadn't.

"Thanks. Have a good night. And thank you for trusting me." I stopped talking because I felt a bubble in the back of my throat. If I didn't stop talking my voice would crack and the tears would fall. I wanted to hug her, but instead I quickly squeezed her hand and gave her a soft, sad smile when she squeezed back.

"Have a good night, Josie."

I marched back to my place and flopped on the couch. What a horrible, life-changing event. Olivia wasn't an ice queen. She was only protecting herself from getting hurt again. That was too much heartache for one lifetime.

I brushed away tears and got ready for bed. I plugged in my phone and crawled under the sheets as another round of sadness washed over me. How was she able to function? Losing a spouse was one thing, but your entire family? I didn't know how she got up every day. This changed everything.

CHAPTER SIX

B rook, you need to come here right now." Cassie stepped aside and waved me in. Their staff bustled around us as they scurried to get ready for the cookout.

I felt completely in the way, and I took a step back when Brook entered the foyer. The portrait of Noah was awkward to hold but I didn't want to set it down with so many people walking through.

"Hi, Jos—Oh, my God. Did you paint this?" Brook asked. At my nod, she continued asking questions. "When did you do this? How? This is incredible."

"Thank you," I said. "I started it earlier in the week. Noah was sweet enough to pose for me. It's dry to the touch but barely. I recommend putting it somewhere where people won't bump it."

"Can we hang it up now? Is that okay?" Cassie asked.

"Of course. If you want to." I handed the canvas to Brook.

Noah joined us and his face lit up. "Is that the portrait? I want to see," he said. Brook turned the portrait so he could see it. "Wow. That's so good. Better than your portrait of Miss Olivia."

I blushed when Brook and Cassie looked at me. I waved them off. "It was a quick sketch in class. We were working on shading." As if that would explain why I sketched our teacher.

"I'm going to put this where people can see it. Thank you again, Josie. This means more to me than you'll ever know," Brook said. She walked off with it with Noah on her heels discussing where they should hang it. I stood there and grinned. Once I realized I was again, literally in the way, I quickly reached for the doorknob.

"I'll see you later. I was a little worried Noah might spill the beans so I wanted to get that to you sooner rather than later. It's my way of thanking you for the grant. It's been a great experience so far."

"It's beautiful. We're going to have to commission you to do one of Ava, too, but we'll talk about that later," Cassie said.

I closed their door feeling incredibly accomplished and grinning from ear to ear. I wanted to fist pump and dance around to release some of the adrenaline from every time they smiled at the portrait. Instead, I headed back to my place to get ready for the party. I sifted through my lean wardrobe and decided on a pair of long tan shorts, a navy blue tank top, and an off-white linen shirt. I knew that once the sun went down, there would be a slight chill. I left the shirt unbuttoned, rolled up the sleeves, and strapped on my sandals.

I assumed Olivia would be at the party. My heart deflated when I thought about what she told me the other night on the beach. I couldn't imagine losing somebody I loved and in such a horrific way.

I pulled out my sketchbook and doodled until the pull of laughter and music was too much and I couldn't stand not being a part of it any longer. I slipped out the back door and climbed the stairs until I was on the massive deck where twenty or so people were milling about. Two bartenders tended a large bar near the patio doors leading into the house. I made a beeline for some liquid courage but stopped when I heard Brook's raspy voice.

"There you are, Josie." She waved me over to a couple and introduced me to them. "This is our artist-in-residence, Josie Lockner. She's the one who gifted us the portrait of Noah that you just admired in the hall. Josie, please meet Robert and Caroline Ashford. Robert handles the legal side of Wellington Enterprises. Caroline is a philanthropist."

"It's nice to meet you both," I said politely.

"It's a beautiful painting of Noah. The way you captured the unique color of his hair and those baby blue eyes. Oh, goodness. Very impressive," Caroline said. She clasped her hands together and smiled fondly at me. She reminded me of my grandmother and I halfway expected her to pinch my cheek.

We shared pleasantries while I learned more about them and tried not to feel incredibly self-conscious at my H&M outfit and sandals that I got at a discount store. Robert was wearing white ankle pants, brown loafers, and a light blue button-down with the sleeves buttoned at his wrists. It was warm and there wasn't a bead of sweat on his body. Caroline was wearing a tulip hem sleeveless salmon dress that hit above her knee and perfectly complemented her husband's outfit. Every so often, a wave of his spicy cologne would waft in the space between us. They both wore sunglasses so it was hard to make a solid connection. I shaded the sun with my hand to see them better.

"We'd love to have you paint our granddaughter. Here, take my card and call me next week. We can discuss it then." Robert handed me a business card that I thanked him for and slipped it into my back pocket.

"I have a few more people that I need to introduce the artist to. Please excuse us," Brook said. She put her arm around my shoulders and gently steered me away. "Don't take less than a thousand for that size. Set your prices accordingly."

My eyes widened at her suggested price, but I nodded. "Thank you for the tip."

"Let's get you a drink and introduce you around," Brook said.

I ordered a gin and tonic and met several other people before Brook was pulled away when Ava started having a meltdown from the people and the noise. I felt her pain. I was at a giant party and knew only the hostesses. I felt underdressed and completely vulnerable. My idea of a cookout was beer, hot dogs, cheeseburgers, chips, and music loud enough to dance to, but low enough to have conversations. This was impressive. The company Brook and Cassie hired did a remarkable job of stringing lights across the deck and creating the perfect beach party ambience for the rich and famous.

"Hey, Josie," Noah said as he and two friends climbed the stairs and approached me.

I smiled at him. "Hey, Noah. What do you have there?"

He held up a net full of shells and sea glass. "Some cool things we found on the beach."

"Nice. Did you go for a swim?"

"Yeah. The water feels good. That's where we found most of the sea glass."

"No sharks?" I asked. "You were careful, right?"

His white-blond hair was wavy from the salt water and his cheeks and the tips of his ears were sunburnt. "We saw a few seals, but no shark fins."

"We're always looking. My brother told us stories about how people got attacked over on Dover Beach." His friend pointed behind them as though I knew where Dover Beach was.

I played along and nodded. "They scare me. Be careful." God, I hated myself for sounding so adult. "But also, have fun."

Noah shaded his eyes with his hand so he could look up at me. "Don't worry. Sharks won't attack in the middle of the day. Only at dusk and dawn when they're hungry. We all know better than to get into the water then." His smile had a hint of indulgence and I couldn't blame him. I literally was there when he returned three books about sharks to the library. He knew way more about sharks than I did.

"You're right, bud. Have a good time." I waited until they passed me before I descended the stairs and headed for the water's edge.

Out of habit, I glanced at the sand dune where Olivia sat night after night, but she wasn't there. It was still the afternoon and for some reason, I believed she only came out here at sunset. I walked along the water's edge until the smell of grilled meats and vegetables was replaced by salty kelp and sea creatures that washed ashore. It smelled like the beach.

I finished my gin and tonic and regretted how far away I was from the Wellingtons. I knew I should have stayed close in case Brook wanted to introduce me to other potential clients, but I felt out of place no matter where I stood. A lone figure coming from the opposite direction mirrored my trek in the soft sand. Sprays of water kicked free with each step. I could tell it was a woman by the floppy straw hat she wore and the dress that wrapped around her knees when the wind picked up. Her hand on her thigh prevented it from moving higher. I smiled when I recognized the form.

"Looks like you could use these."

Olivia handed me her sunglasses. I tried to wave her off, but she insisted. "I have a hat. I don't need both and I can't stress enough how important it is for young people to wear sunglasses. Aging's a bitch."

"Thank you. I was ill-prepared for this impromptu walk." My heart picked up speed when our fingers touched as she handed me the glasses. I slipped the oversized frames on my face and felt instant relief. "Also, you can't be that much older than I am." She gave me a look that said I was full of shit. "Well, however old you are, you look amazing."

The brim of her floppy hat lifted in the wind when she shook her head and smiled. "Flattery will get you everywhere. You're what? Twenty-two?"

I felt a small jolt at her teasing. "Twenty-three. And a half."

She laughed and it made my heart race all over again. I knew she was thirty-five. Most of the women I'd dated were older, but only by a year or two. And why was I thinking of her that way? Olivia was grieving a massive loss. She needed a friend, not a crush.

"Have you been to the party, yet?" I asked.

"I thought I'd go for a walk and wait for more people to show up," she said.

She looked so carefree and relaxed. It was the first time I'd seen a full smile on her face in days. It warmed my heart. This was a different Olivia. I touched her arm as my way of saying hello and to feel that she was really here in front of me.

"I did the same thing. I felt so out of place there. I only know Brook, Cassie, the kids, and you. They're busy so I think you're stuck with me for a bit." I didn't tell her that Brook introduced me to several people whose names I couldn't recall. I wanted to spend time with her.

"I don't think that's a bad thing. Do you?"

I swore she winked at me but nothing else on her face indicated that she was flirting. Plus, we had a pretty emotionally charged night that last time we spoke. She confused me. "I think it's a great thing." I shoved my hands in my pockets to keep from nervously twirling my hair. "How was your day?"

"Good. I sold a sculpture and shut down the gallery early because I knew everyone would be here." Olivia had to keep one hand on her dress to keep the wind from blowing it up around her waist. Her fingers were long and the tips were painted a soft pink. Today was the first day I'd seen her without any jewelry.

"I'll have to visit again soon. You have nice pieces beside your own." I cringed knowing I was fangirling. I just wanted to spend more time with her.

"Any time you want to stop by. I have two new paintings you might like." She bit her bottom lip as though she was thinking, but the way her teeth scraped slowly across her bottom lip was so damn sexy.

I cleared my throat. "I'll swing by next week." I was very aware of the lack of space between us, but Olivia didn't seem to be. I briefly glanced down where the soft swell of her breasts peeked out from the vee of her dress. She caught my eyes traveling down her body. I blushed when she raised her eyebrow knowingly at me. I shrugged. I wasn't sorry and she didn't seem to mind. I quickly changed the subject. "I don't know about you but I'm ready to eat." My stomach rumbled at the smells coming from the three giant grills.

"I haven't eaten today so I'm with you," she said.

"Were you not hungry?" I didn't want to pry.

"I painted this morning. I barely made it to the gallery to open up on time. I forgot about eating," she said. It was so refreshing to be around another artist who completely understood what it was like to get lost in creating something.

"Same. I was finishing up my present for Brook and Cassie." I moved to the side as a group of people made their way down the stairs as we were climbing up. My hand brushed Olivia's back when I reached for the railing as I slipped in step behind her. "Sorry," I mumbled.

"Quit apologizing. You're fine." She was two steps ahead of me and when she turned, we were the same height. I watched as her gaze traveled my face and lingered over my lips. It took everything I had not to wet them with my tongue. Not in a seductive way, but in a suddenly my mouth is dry and I'm very nervous to be this close to this much beauty way. "What did you paint for them?"

I moved two steps up so that I was beside her. I towered over her by at least five inches. She had to look up. I never noticed the small flecks of amber in her brown eyes. I liked how the sun made them sparkle. "A portrait of Noah."

"I'd love to see it." Her voice was warm, and I swear she was leaning toward me.

I nervously tucked a chunk of hair that had slid out of my ponytail behind my ear. The smirk that settled on her full mouth indicated that she knew exactly what she was doing to me. "It's not a big deal." I wanted her to see it, but then I didn't. "It's why I missed class." That was only half-true.

"Speaking of which, I'm going to reimburse you for the class."

"No. Absolutely not. I committed but failed. It's not your fault."

She put her hands on her hips. "You didn't learn anything in my class."

"That's not true," I said. She gave me that look again. I smiled in surrender. "How about splitting it? I mean, you gave us really nice sketchpads that I know weren't cheap." It was ridiculous that I was arguing about a few hundred dollars with a millionaire. I needed that money and she knew it. She was being kind and I was being ridiculous. Olivia pulled out her phone and ten seconds later, I had two hundred dollars back.

"There. I kept twenty-nine dollars for supplies. End of discussion. Let's grab a drink and a plate of food."

"Thank you." It wasn't worth keeping the argument up. I was proud, but not stupid. I followed her around forking chunks of fruit and barbecued meats on my plate. "Is it terrible that I'll probably make three trips up here to eat everything I want?" Olivia's plate had about half of what mine did.

"You still have a youthful metabolism. Eat as much as you want," Olivia said. She was completely hung up on age and I didn't know why. Thirty-five wasn't old. She was beautiful, sexy, successful, and even though she lost so much, her life was far from over.

I took a different approach. "Well, since neither of us ate today, let's just enjoy it. Can I get you a glass of wine or a beer?" There were pitchers of ice water on the tables, as well as the caterers running around to refill glasses with iced tea and lemonade.

"A beer sounds perfect."

"I'll be right back." The bar had about fifteen different longnecks that I didn't recognize and a few I did. "I'll take two Sam Adams." The icy bottles almost slipped from my hands as I made my way back to our table. I couldn't wait to take a sip. The liquid courage would help settle my nerves. When I got back to the table, I found the Ashfords were sitting with Olivia.

Caroline waved to me. "There she is."

"Olivia, did you see Josie's portrait? It's wonderful. We want to commission Josie to paint our granddaughter," Robert said.

I forced a smile. While it was flattering that they sought me out, I really wanted alone time with Olivia. We had a budding friendship since she revealed her emotional scars and I wanted to know more. While I was obviously attracted to her, I was also genuinely interested in her life.

"Not yet. I'll have to check it out," Olivia said.

"You know, maybe you can hang some of Josie's work in your gallery when you do the end of the summer show," Robert said.

I picked at the label of my beer, wishing I could slip between the planks of wood like sand and blow away from this uncomfortable conversation. Their intentions were good, but their timing was horrible.

"That's a strong possibility," Olivia said.

"Oh, you don't have to. I don't really have a lot to display." I felt the heat flame out from my cheeks and took a long pull from my beer. I finally took a bite of dinner when Robert turned his attention to his wife.

"Noah's portrait must be very impressive," Olivia said.

I swallowed hard trying to dislodge the piece of chicken that clung to my throat at her words. I reached for my beer to help it down and covered my mouth with my hand. "It's not. I mean, it's good, but it was just something I painted in a short time." It was great, but I was talking to one of my idols and had to downplay it. What if she hated it? "It was just a quick thank you gift."

"Let's finish up here and take a look at it."

"Or we can just grab two more beers and head to the beach and forget about it. We could go for another walk." That seemed to be our thing. Or I was trying to make it our thing. I liked spending time with her.

"Too late. The band's setting up. It's going to be hard to get to the beach until after they're done." Olivia pointed to the stage I saw workers erect earlier in the week. Three stagehands set up drums, a guitar, a bass, and extra microphones. I saw a group of grungy looking guys lingering in a corner of the deck and more blocking the steps.

"Wait. Is that Fast Cars?" I was shocked that the Wellingtons landed such a huge name for their party.

"Yep. They never disappoint with the entertainment. Fast Cars is from here and they do this concert every year if they aren't on tour. Somehow one of the band members is related to Brook."

She pointed to the drummer who was waving his drumsticks at a couple sitting at a table near the stage. "I think that's Brook's sister-in-law's nephew, or something like that. His name is Karson. He spent most of his summers here when he was a kid."

"They're going to be loud, aren't they?" I asked. I only knew a handful of songs by them and only a few were slow. They were mainstream, but heavy on the rock side. She nodded.

"They won't be the only performers. They'll have at least three different groups or musicians play."

"So, it's like Godapalooza." It took her a few seconds to get my joke and her delightful laugh filled my ears and made me want to hear it again.

"I guess you could call it that. Only it's for four hours, there's plenty of space to dance, plenty of food to eat, lots of alcohol, and a solid shelter if it storms."

"Sounds a lot more fun than Lalapalooza."

"It's been a long time since I've done anything like that," Olivia said.

I wasn't going to tease her because I had a feeling the reason was her family, and I didn't want to bring them up while she was obviously having a good time. "I did a three-day festival in upstate New York and vowed never again."

"That bad, huh?"

"Maybe I'm spoiled, but access to fresh water and food, not drugs, is a better experience for me. I'd rather see the musicians I like in single concerts, not weekend events where you camp and then can't find your way back." There was that laugh again. I nodded. "Yeah, it took me two hours to find my tent because hundreds of other people decided to buy an orange two-person tent."

"Did you go with friends?"

Confession time. "I went with my girlfriend. Well, ex-girlfriend now." I looked at her for any sort of surprise, but her expression remained passive. "We broke up after that concert."

"Do you have a girlfriend now? Or boyfriend?" she asked. I shook my head.

"No girlfriend. I've avoided relationships before the program because I didn't want any distractions. My whole goal here is to become more proficient with my creative expression and make connections. I didn't want to have to worry about splitting my time between my passion for art and, well, other passions."

She held up a finger playfully. "Speaking of passions, why don't we go check out Noah's portrait and then grab maybe wine instead of beer and head to the beach?" She wasn't going to let me off the hook.

I waved her off. "Or we can skip the portrait, grab wine and head to the beach."

"You're nervous about me seeing the painting. You're very good. I can't imagine it's bad."

"I know you think I didn't learn anything in class, but I did. The way you talked about color theory really made sense to me. I know it was a beginner class, but none of my art teachers ever talked about color the way you did. This is hard for me because I'm standing in front of one of my idols."

She stared at me so long, but I wasn't going to show her that it bothered me. I dug my fingernails into my palms and stared back. Her eyes were stunning. Her lashes were long and her skin was smooth. I wondered if she felt as soft as she looked. For the first time, she seemed embarrassed by my praise. She looked away.

"Thank you. Now about your painting…" she paused. Her shyness empowered me.

"Let's go."

CHAPTER SEVEN

We could hear the music just fine from the little sand dune on the beach. A bottle of wine was nestled in the sand between us. Olivia had stashed two small beach chairs against the dune that I didn't notice the first time I strolled down here. It was as though she knew this would happen at some point tonight. I didn't question it. I rolled down my sleeves to stay warm while she poured the first glass. It was in the lower seventies, but with my sunburn and the soft breeze from the water, I was cold. I couldn't believe she was fine wearing a short-sleeved top.

"Aren't you cold?" I asked.

"No. Cold doesn't usually get to me." She handed me a plastic glass.

"Classy." I frowned at the plastic stem but understood the need for it. Nobody wanted to cut their foot on broken glass while taking a beach stroll.

I took a sip and pretended my heart wasn't racing as I waited for her to talk about the portrait. If this chair would've allowed me to be sitting on its edge, I would have been perched waiting for her critique. Ten minutes ago, when she stood three feet from the portrait, I grabbed a bottle of rosé from the bar and waited for her at the top of the stairs. It took every ounce of my willpower to not race over there and tell her everything I would do differently or how I would've used more yellow in his hair or made his smile a little less *Mona Lisa*-like.

Olivia sat and stared out at the ocean. "Your patience is amazing."

"Secretly, I'm dying inside. Or maybe not so secretly." I smiled at her and quirked my eyebrow.

"Okay, here it is. The honest truth."

I blew out a deep breath and nodded. "I'm ready."

"It's wonderful." Her voice was soft and held the hint of a smile.

"Really?"

"You're very talented. I love the use of different colors for a solid."

I interrupted her. "I learned that from studying your work." I covered my mouth. "Sorry. I didn't mean to interrupt." I needed her words and soaked in her approval.

"It's lovely." She paused as though recalling the painting in her head. "You've captured his intelligence in his eyes. You painted his innocence even though he's teetering on the brink of changes. I understand why Brook and Cassie love it."

My heart soared. It was as though a celebratory bottle of champagne exploded inside me and bubbles of excitement poured through my veins. I wanted to do cartwheels in the sand. Instead, I leaned back in the chair and bit the insides of my cheeks to keep myself from grinning too hard.

"Thank you." I waited a few moments before I sprung my idea on her. "I came here to paint landscapes. They've always been my focus, but the portrait unlocked something in me. I know portraits are your specialty. Would you be willing to mentor me? I'm sure I could learn a lot from you. I could help you out by working in the gallery as payment."

I looked at her silhouette against the darkening sky. She chewed on her bottom lip as she thought about my offer. I took another sip of wine to both calm my nerves and prove that I could be chill. Fast Cars had finished their set and a woman with a guitar was on stage. I could hear the hard strumming of each chord.

"You don't have to work at the gallery, but I would be willing to help you work on your craft," she said.

I bounced with excitement. "I can't ask you to do this for free. Let me do something as payment like help paint the inside of your house or do your grocery shopping. I'll even run to the dry cleaners. Consider me your personal assistant."

She touched my hand. "I don't need an assistant, but thanks for the offer. I'm sure we can come up with something later. Maybe you can take me to dinner as a thank you."

I barely heard her words because her hand was on mine for a solid ten seconds before she pulled away. I hit replay in my mind to confirm she really said I could take her to dinner as a thank you before I responded. "I would love to take you to dinner." Never mind the part about her agreeing to be my mentor.

She quirked her eyebrow. "Dinner as friends."

Feeling playful and getting the same vibe from her, I put my hand on my heart. "Of course. I wouldn't have it any other way. But I think you might be flirting with me."

"You're my student. It would be inappropriate to flirt with you." She smiled at me over the rim of her plastic glass before taking a small sip. She took my breath away.

I had to tell myself to blink. And to breathe. And to smile and laugh as though my heart wasn't pounding and the blood heating my veins wasn't lava. Knowing that saying anything more was pushing it, I switched topics. "Thank you for being my mentor. I promise to be a good student." I mentally high-fived myself over everything that had happened over the last two minutes.

She settled back in her chair and my stress level floated away when I realized I had said the right thing. "When did you know you were an artist?" she asked.

I drew my knees up to my chest and dusted the sand from my feet. I couldn't believe this moment was happening. Two months ago, I was living off energy drinks and knock-off Oreos. Sleep was a catnap here and there while I worked on final projects. Now, I was at a massive beach party, eating delicious gourmet food, and rubbing elbows with some of the richest people in the country. And I was sitting beside O. Colburn. It felt surreal. I looked at Olivia. She had taken off her hat and pulled her long hair over her shoulder. She was breathtaking.

"When I could hold a pencil or piece of chalk. What about you?" I smiled thinking back to the chalk drawings on my parents' driveway and how the local news covered it. It was a feel-good filler piece and had been viewed over a million times on YouTube. It was one of the six things on my YouTube channel before I abandoned it because I wanted to spend all my time drawing and painting.

"Believe it or not, I was a late bloomer. It was middle school for me. I doodled a lot and one of my teachers told me I should try some art classes. I went to a visual arts high school and graduated from Rhode Island like you did. You have natural talent. Mine is learned," Olivia said.

That was the biggest compliment I could've ever expected from anyone. I stayed silent, afraid that if I spoke, I would ruin the magic. I nodded when she lifted the bottle and watched as she gracefully poured more wine into our glasses.

"Thank you. What've you've learned to do has been incredible. What was the first thing you ever sold?"

"The first thing I sold to a stranger on my own and not through the school was a painting of Boston," she said.

I loved that she was opening up to me. I went from what seemed like her least favorite person to a friend. Or at least the beginning of a friendship. I liked Olivia. She was smart, artistic, successful as a businesswoman and an artist, had great hair, and a sexy body. But I didn't give myself permission to crush because she had so much pain in her heart. That wasn't fair to either one of us.

"Was it that piece in the Wroughton Museum in Boston? I love the reflection of the city in the water. Everything was so detailed. I remember how you could see the addresses and street names in the reflection." I sighed appreciatively recalling that piece of art. "I love that you don't just paint the beach," I said.

"I'm flattered that you know my work so well."

"There are so many instructors who still use your work as examples. It's incredible." Fangirling wasn't my thing, and I regretted the words as soon as they left my mouth. I could practically see her walls return. I quickly switched gears. "Do you want to go on a walk?" I needed to walk off the alcohol. I was getting too comfortable sitting with Olivia and I didn't need liquor to loosen my lips.

"Josie! Mom's looking for you." Noah and the two friends glued to his side found us. Worst timing ever, little dude. I wanted to shoo him away, but I couldn't blame him. He couldn't read my mind or know what was happening.

My shoulders sank because I knew my time on the beach with Olivia was over. I was sure Brook was looking for me to introduce me to other potential clients. I understood why she was so successful at her job. She was a bulldog even about something as little as finding me work. I appreciated her help, but right now I just wanted to spend time with Olivia.

"Go on. I'll catch up. I'm going to make a quick stop at my house and then I'll be over," Olivia said.

"See you there," I said, not really knowing if that was true or not.

Olivia wasn't a crowd-loving person. The deck and the beach were packed with people, and I knew this would be the last time I would see her tonight. Just when we were getting comfortable talking about her art. I admired so much about Olivia, but I wasn't sure where I stood with her. Did she see me as just a curious student or a woman who was interested in her? She was standoffish, but then almost flirty at times. That confused me. With anyone else, I would flirt back, but Olivia was so damaged that I didn't want to upset our budding friendship. She was beginning to trust me and I didn't want to fracture that. My instincts told me to go ahead and flirt back but read her mood first. It could backfire, but it could also open the door to something stronger than friendship. Earlier, she caught me staring at her cleavage and didn't seem bothered by it. I was going to have to tread carefully but I gave myself the green light, which made me even sadder that I probably wouldn't see her again tonight.

Noah walked beside me while his friends shadowed us on our way back to the house. It was nice to see him interact with friends his own age.

"I heard you helped pick the musicians," I said.

He thumbed one of the kids behind him. "Jacob is Karson's brother. You know, the drummer. They always play at our party. Mom is friends with the other people who play. I don't know them very well," he said.

"Over here, Josie." Brook's clipped voice got my immediate attention. She introduced me to more guests who were impressed with the painting.

I knew it was wise to be present in the moment, but I wanted to get back to Olivia. After an hour of scanning the crowd every two minutes, it was apparent she wasn't coming back. I chatted with Cassie and danced with Ava. She was having a hard time sleeping with all the noise, so I danced with her until she drifted off to sleep. Cassie peeled her off my chest and disappeared with her.

Even though the party was in full swing, I needed to get away. After shaking hands and collecting cards, I went back to my place to decompress. Back at my place, I spread out the business cards of potential clients. I was so excited that I had leads. When I came here, I imagined people would pluck my art up at a street fair for fifty dollars a pop—barely enough to cover supplies. I never thought I'd get commissioned work right out of the gate. Applying for this grant was the best thing to ever happen to me.

CHAPTER EIGHT

"Thank you for doing this," I said. I followed Olivia into her house and gasped with glee when a tabby cat jumped on the foyer table to greet me. "Hi, kitty. Oh, look at you. Aren't you just the sweetest thing?" I was hyper-aware that this was her private space, and just being here set me on edge. She seemed softer here. The tabby sniffed my hand.

Olivia smiled at our exchange. "Meet Cuddles. He's the greeting committee."

I leaned closer and rubbed his chin. Deep rumbles immediately rolled through his chest and bubbled up into his throat. "Hello, Cuddles. What an adorable name." I missed cats. My college roommate had one who liked to snuggle with me late at night. I was sadder to say good-bye to Meowvin than the roommate.

"My daughter named him. He was either going to be Cuddles or Kitty."

My anxiety grew when she mentioned her daughter. I didn't know if I was allowed to ask questions about her or not. "Well, he seems to be very cuddly so she did a good job."

She raised her eyebrow at me. "My studio is in the back of the house. In the future, you can just knock on the back door on the days we're scheduled to work together. I rarely hear the doorbell back here." She motioned for me to follow her to her studio.

I tried not to look at her bare legs, but fuck, it was hard. She was wearing shorts, a cotton T-shirt, and a long sleeve shirt that was dotted with different colors and types of dried paint. Her casualness blew me away. When she threw her hair up in a bun as we weaved through the living room and kitchen, I almost fainted. It was a simple move, but it was so sexy. This was no longer a harmless crush. The woman in front of me gave me sparks that burned hot in my stomach.

"Your house is beautiful," I said. It was stunning. And big. Too big for just her.

"Thank you." She pushed the double doors open to her studio and I stopped to soak it all in.

"Oh, my God! This studio is amazing. Tell me you live here year-round." Most of the houses in Goda were empty shells during the winter months. I didn't give her a chance to answer. "Because I would never leave this place." I did a slow walk around the large room with floor to ceiling windows and dark mahogany wood floors. The lighting was impressive.

"I spend the winters in Boston, but I hold off as long as I can because this feels like home," she said.

For so many reasons, I thought. Even though I wanted to spend at least an hour going through her supplies and equipment, I refrained and stood by one of the two easels she had set up.

"Feel free to move it wherever you want," she said.

"What are we drawing or painting?" I rolled up and down on the balls of my feet, waiting for her to answer. I was so freaking excited to be here, in this moment, with this artist. Learning from her was a dream come true.

"What do you want to work on?"

That was a good question. I thought for a few moments while she patiently waited for my answer. "I want to know how to capture emotions better in portraits and I know you do that really well. Portraiture was never on my radar until I got here. The process is challenging and the outcome, so far, has been rewarding. I know Noah so capturing his personality wasn't hard. What happens when I don't know my subject? I have a stack of business cards of people who want portraits of their kids and pets. How do I do that if I don't know them?" I heard panic in my voice. Olivia walked over to me, took my hands, and shook them so that my arms were loose. "What are you doing?"

She stopped shaking so now we just were holding hands in the middle of her studio. Her fingers were warm but firm. "First lesson is you need to relax. Maybe take a few deep breaths." She breathed deeply and exhaled slowly waiting for me to mimic her. After three deep breaths, my heart was finally at a reasonable pace. "Better?" she asked. At my nod, she dropped my hands.

"You said you had somebody who wanted you to draw their pet?"

"Is that weird? Should I have turned them down?"

She waved me off. "Not unless you're uncomfortable doing it. You're going to get the most ridiculous requests especially if your clients are rich. Very rich means they can afford to be eccentric. It happens a lot."

"No, I like animals." I threw my hands up. "But how do I get to know the personality of a pet?"

"Hang on. I'll be right back."

She returned with Cuddles thrown over one shoulder. He was still sleeping. She gently placed him on a cushion by one of the windows. "What can you tell me about Cuddles?"

I froze. I didn't know anything about her cat. "Um. He likes to sleep. And he's friendly."

She gently raked her fingers across his orange and white fur. His purrs got louder and he stretched into a more comfortable position. "So, I recommend talking to the people who commission you. Find out why they want a portrait. Have them tell you stories about that person or pet."

I sat next to Cuddles. "Okay, Olivia. What can you tell me about Cuddles? Has he always been an indoor cat? How did he come to be a member of your family? Was he a rescue? A stray?"

She tilted her head and smiled. "Exactly. It's an interview. It's your observation as well as the information you gather to help find the emotions you want to convey."

"So, what are your answers?"

"He's the bestest boy ever. He was a street stray. A friend of mine found him and three other kittens in a box by a dumpster. Even though Miranda was a toddler, he really took to her. He was protective of her since day one." Pain and a sad smile flickered across her face. It was obvious she was remembering moments with Miranda and Cuddles. I focused my attention on the cat because I didn't know what to say. He was a safe subject.

I ran my thumb over his pink toes. "He doesn't mind that?"

Olivia shook her head. "Miranda used to drag him around like a rag doll and he just took it. Nothing bothers him at all."

"Truly the bestest boy," I said.

"Let's start off with simple sketching. Pets are hard. People are easy."

I snorted. "Sure."

"He's really the only model we have at the moment," she said. That wasn't true. I could draw her, but then she would want to draw me and I wasn't ready for that scrutiny. Not from her. She pulled out a sketchpad and I panicked when I saw my name on it in bold, block letters. It was from her class. "Here's your sketchpad."

I almost snatched it from her hands. I thought she had given it to Noah so I hadn't given it any thought. She either saw the charcoal sketch and wasn't impressed or respected my privacy and didn't look. That was incredible willpower. I would've looked.

"Oh, thanks." I flipped it open to a clean page and waited for instruction.

"He won't move from this position." She angled Cuddles so that his sleeping face was pointed at me. "We've got him like this for about two hours."

I opened my pencil case and selected a pencil. When she started drawing so confidently, so boldly, I stopped to watch her. I asked several questions before I worked up enough courage to start. I moved my easel closer to hers, careful not to disturb Cuddles and by the end of our session, I had pretty good bones of a drawing that looked like him and not just a sketch of one.

"You're a quick study," she said.

I tried not to beam like a happy child. "Thank you. I've always loved private lessons. You can learn so much more than if you're in a classroom sharing the instructor's attention." I watched as she put away her supplies. I wasn't ready to end our evening even though the lesson was over. "Would you like to grab dinner somewhere?" She turned and looked at me so sharply that I thought I offended her. I took a step back. "I owe you dinner and I just thought since neither one of us has eaten yet, we could grab something in town." I tried to look casually bored.

"It's been a long day."

"Come on. Friends have dinner. Plus, that was part of the agreement." I packed away my pencils and waited for either her explanation or her excuse why we shouldn't. She twisted a button on her shirt while she thought about my offer. I held my breath afraid to exhale.

"Okay. We can go to Remington's. It's still open."

I looked down at the denim shirt I was wearing to protect my sundress in case we used oil paints. I didn't look too horrible. I took off the shirt and folded it over my arm.

"I need to change. The world can't see me like this," Olivia said.

"You look amazing."

She blushed and waved me off. "Give me five minutes."

"Booooo."

A smile joined the blush and she excused herself. I stroked Cuddles until she returned. He was super chill and I thought Olivia might have exaggerated about him being awake four hours out of the day. When she returned, I was the one who felt inadequate. Her hair was down, her makeup touched up, and she was wearing a cream-colored dress that showed off her curves. It wasn't super casual and suddenly this one hundred percent felt like a date.

"Forget the booooo. I approve." I hoped my smile wasn't as cheesy as it felt. "Wait. Am I underdressed?"

She gave me a full up-and-down look and shot me a smile that I hadn't seen before. It was sexy and unleashed a kaleidoscope of butterflies in my stomach. "You look fine. Since you're already here, I'll drive," she said. She cleared her throat of the huskiness that had settled there. I refused to read into it.

I was thankful she offered to drive and hoped my sigh of relief wasn't audible. My car wasn't nice enough for anybody older than twelve. The air conditioning was wonky and there was a musty smell that couldn't be identified. But also, I didn't care enough to look for the source until now.

"That would be great." I followed her to the garage and climbed into the passenger seat of her two-seater BMW. It was a struggle. I slid the seat all the way back because I was all legs.

"I know this isn't a practical car, but it's fun," she said.

The space got small once I shut the door. I was very aware of how close we sat and how our arms brushed every time she shifted. "I can't drive a manual shift."

"What? It's the only way to drive a car like this," she said. I liked the way the sunset cascaded warm colors into the car and settled gently across her face. Her voice was light and soft. Her car was a place of comfort for her. I noticed how relaxed she seemed the second we drove off. "Looks like I'll have something else to teach you, too." I took it as an innuendo even if she didn't intend it that way.

I paused for a few seconds. "I don't think I'll ever drive one."

"Are you scared of a little car?" she asked.

"I'm scared of an expensive little car." I emphasized "expensive" because that was what really scared me.

"I'm insured."

"Okay. But not tonight. I need my brain to relax."

"I get that." She pulled into the parking lot of Remington's and slipped into a small spot near the entrance. "And this is why I have a little car for driving in town." She grinned. Smiling Olivia was so refreshing. In this moment, her tragic loss wasn't present in the space between us.

"That's exactly why I have a small car, too. They are easier to park."

"Have you eaten here before?" she asked.

I almost snorted. Like all the restaurants in Goda, menus were posted outside. I remember reading the menu from this restaurant and realizing the only thing I could afford was a side salad. "No, I've only been to one restaurant in Goda. Down the street." I thumbed behind me too embarrassed to say the name because it was more of a cheap walk-up, whereas Remington's was obviously four stars. The linen tablecloths, flickering flames on candles, and classical music played low made me feel completely out of my element, but I couldn't let Olivia know.

"Hello, Olivia. It's nice to see you again," an older gentleman said as he approached with his hands out.

Olivia squeezed his hands and air-kissed his cheek. "It's good to be back. I've missed your food." She turned to me. "This is Josie. She's here for the summer. Josie, this is Charles. Remington's is his restaurant."

He gave me a warm smile. "It's a pleasure to meet you." He turned to Olivia after I shook his hand. "Let's get you a good table." He brought us to a booth that overlooked the ocean, gave us menus, and left quietly.

"So, what's good here?" I looked at the menu like I was going to eat anything other than salad.

"If you like seafood, you can't go wrong with the special." Our waiter put a basket of bread on the table and offered us the wine list. "We'll take a bottle of the Machard Gramont Pinot Noir." Olivia handed him back the list without even consulting me and it was hot the way she took control. "I hope that's okay."

I felt like a deer in headlights. Olivia, with her walls down, was fire. I didn't know what I did to get her to open up to me, but I wasn't going to jinx it. "I'm leaving my fate in your hands." And awkward me was back. "I mean, I trust you."

"How much do you trust me?" she asked.

"All the way." I nodded thinking it was just a random question given that we were at a restaurant.

"Do you mind if I order for us?"

I stared at her, wondering if the two hundred she refunded was enough to cover the meal. I tried to relax the flutter of panic that crept up and stopped right before it jumped into my throat. "Yes, of course."

"And don't worry. This is my treat." She turned toward the returning waiter before I could protest. She rattled off an order in French and I was frozen in my seat because she sounded so sexy and in charge. I didn't recognize anything she asked for, but I trusted her completely.

The waiter nodded his approval and poured our wine. I nervously took a sip. She wasn't wrong. It was delicious.

Was I grateful or upset? I invited her and fully planned to pay. "Thanks. Also, I can pay. It was my treat."

She held her hand up to stop me. "You're my guest and I insist. Besides, Charles and I go way back." I obviously had the worst poker face because she touched my hand briefly. "You can treat next time."

I mustered a smile. "Okay." At least she said there was going to be a next time.

"How has your time in Goda been so far?" she asked. It was good question to slip us into an easy conversation that wasn't setting either one of us on edge.

"It's everything and more. I adore the Wellingtons. I love that they are two women who found love and got married." I learned a long time ago not to assume labels. I didn't know how they identified. "Have you known them a long time?"

"I've had the summer house about ten years now. Brook was married to a different woman at the time, but I've known her family for a decade now." She gently tapped her fingertips on the stem of her wineglass. Her nails were trimmed and painted rich copper. I wondered how often she changed their color. I was never more self-conscious of my hands than right now.

"I love their story. It's very romantic," I said.

"They're a great couple. They were there for me when I lost my husband and daughter." She paused and I looked away for a moment to give her privacy to collect herself. "It's good that your portrait of Noah was a hit. Brook has a lot of connections, and you'll get a lot of work," she said.

"That's why I'm here. To build a clientele and be as famous as the once mysterious O. Colburn."

She wrinkled her nose at me and groaned. "Not so mysterious anymore."

"You're still mysterious, but I like that I'm getting to know you. As an artist and as a woman." It couldn't hurt to throw that out there. She already knew that I identified as a lesbian and I'd flirted with her. Plus, I was pretty sure she had flirted back. As long as I wasn't making her feel uncomfortable, I was going to keep dropping hints. "Speaking of, when did you open the gallery?"

"Seven years ago."

"I'm so curious about people who have two different residences. What's happens during the winter? What do you do with the art? Does it stay down here?"

She shook her head. "I close from mid-December until April first. Everything is online so it's still a working gallery. The art is transported to my place in Boston during winter because if it sells, I can ship it out from there."

"I can't help but be impressed by you." I clinked my glass against hers which brought out another smile. "Thank you for opening up to me and being my friend." I knew I put her on the spot, but deep down, I thought she needed somebody in her life who wasn't a reminder of the past.

CHAPTER NINE

It was two in the morning when I heard knocking on my studio door. I jolted out of bed and flung open the door.

Olivia was leaning against the doorframe. "You're not answering your phone."

My hand went to my heart to calm its racing. "You scared the crap out of me." I hissed out an angry breath when I realized there wasn't an emergency.

"We need to talk," she said. She slid by me without an invitation and sat on the only chair in the studio.

"Let's go in the living room so we can both sit," I said.

"I know it's late, but I figured you'd still be up." She pointed her finger at me and moved it up and down. "You should probably put on more clothes."

I turned on a light. "Well, since you woke me up at my place, I don't think you really have a say in what I wear." I put my hands on my hips, emphasizing my stance on her rudeness. I was wearing a tank and thin boxers and she was lucky I was wearing anything at all. I stared at her hard. Something had changed and I didn't like it.

"You're very distracting at the moment. Will you please put on a robe or something?" she asked.

"Fine. Have a seat. I'll be right back." I raced to the bedroom and grabbed a hoodie. What was she doing here? My boxers scrunched up inside the leggings I pulled on. I slipped my hands inside to straighten out the seams.

She smiled when I walked into the room. "Nice look."

"Does it really matter? That's what I sleep in. You asked me to cover up so I did." I wasn't about to adjust my boxers again even though I was uncomfortable.

She stood and looked uncomfortable for the first time. "I'm sorry about waking you. I figured you were awake because the studio light was on. I just wanted you to know that I have to cancel our lessons."

"Like tomorrow? I'm glad you're here, but you could've just texted me." I stifled a yawn. The initial adrenaline left my body and I was left with a need to curl up and go back to sleep.

She stood. "I mean all of them. I can't mentor you anymore. Look, Josie. I saw what you did."

"What? What are you talking about? What did I do?" I wracked my brain trying to figure out what I'd done or said that would've put her over the edge. Especially at this hour. "We've only had four lessons and I'm already learning so much from you." We spent all week drawing faces. I had started a self-portrait that I loathed, but she made me push through the discomfort of drawing what I saw as my flaws. She told me nobody had the perfect face, but she was wrong. She did.

Olivia blew out a deep, very audible breath. "I saw the drawing you did of me."

My heart flatlined. My breath disappeared, or maybe I held it. Either way, I was struggling. I could handle this bomb one of two ways. I opted for the one that didn't make me look like a creeper.

"Oh, that?" I waved my hand at her like it wasn't a big deal. "That was just practice. I hardly knew you then. You said we could draw anything in the room and I took you literally." I sat in the chair opposite her and tried to look as bored as I could. My heart picked up speed at the look she shot me.

"You did it without my permission."

Drawing Olivia without her permission was a bonehead move that I started out of spite, but finished because she was so inspiring and beautiful. It felt like a calling and I didn't regret it even if I did it without her knowing. "I didn't think it was bad."

"Oh, I never said it was. It was inappropriate. You know what the difference is, right?"

The heat on my cheeks told her that I knew. "I don't even know what to say." I wasn't embarrassed by the quality, because I knew it turned out well. "Wait. Why were you looking at my sketchpad?"

It was her turn to blush. "I just wanted to see your progress." She folded her arms and stared at me.

I could've pounced and made her feel guilty for looking, but deep down, I wanted her to see it. I wanted her approval. I always had. "What did you think of your portrait?"

Her body language changed with each emotion that washed over her. The roller coaster my heart was on needed to stop. "From an instructor's standpoint, it's good. It's in proportion, it looks like me. From a friend's perspective, you should have asked."

Maybe I was pushing it, but this was about more than art. "Olivia, do you mind if I draw you?" I put my elbows on my knees and steepled my fingers to rest against my chin while she thought about my question. She seemed taken aback that I would even ask it, but I had nothing to lose. "At least finish what I started?" Her shoulders dropped and I knew she was caving. I smiled a cheesy, lopsided grin.

"One night. I'll give you one night." Her voice was low and quiet and for a brief moment, I wondered what she meant by those words.

I sat up straighter and looked into her eyes but they were still angry so I proceeded with caution. "I only need a few hours," I said. I poured us both a glass of water to break the tension in the room.

"How are you able to knock down my walls?" she asked.

"Because you don't expect anything from me. I'm not perceived as a threat." I didn't even try to hide the fact that I was watching her lick her lips after every sip of water. Something was happening between us. She took the initiative to come here and didn't act like she was leaving any time soon. I wanted her here.

She tilted her head and pursed her lips. "You know what? You're right."

"Let's talk about something else. Tell me about your life in Boston."

"It's just like it is here only there's no beach."

"Who's your best friend?" I asked.

She crossed her legs and leaned back in her chair. "His name is Michael."

"Oh? How long has he been your best friend?"

"Since college. And no, we've never dated. He's gay."

I held up my hands defensively. "I didn't mean anything by my line of questioning. I'm sure it gets lonely for you. I just wanted to know if you had a friend in the city who helps get you through the tough times."

"I have neighbors, friends, and a therapist. I'm fine. Really."

I leaned closer. "What about here? Who do you have here?"

"How did this conversation turn into all about me? I came here to ask why you drew me and suddenly it's an inquisition."

Here went nothing. "I drew you because you're beautiful. And you're challenging." I twirled my hand in a circular motion around her face. "There are so many emotions on your face at any given moment and I was drawn to you because of how vulnerable you are. Before I even knew your history." I was on edge because I thought I'd said too much.

She bowed her head. "You are very young."

I wasn't expecting her to bring up my age right now. "So? I don't know what that means and how that relates to you. Or to us. You can't tell me you don't have friends who are twelve or fifteen years older than you."

"Friends, huh?"

"Yeah. We do friend things. We've shared meals, had long walks together. You've told me your heartaches. Of course, I'm your friend." I was confused.

"But sometimes you don't look at me like I'm a friend."

I took her hands in mine. "I'm your friend."

"But you're attracted to me." Her voice wasn't accusatory or angry. It was matter-of-fact. She didn't let go of my hands either.

"Yes, I am. I thought the flirting was harmless. But I'll stop if it makes you uncomfortable."

She squeezed my fingers before pulling away. "It doesn't make me uncomfortable. It's not like you're the first woman who has flirted with me."

"Oh, yeah?" My pulse quickened at what my brain was trying to process.

"I did date before I got married you know," she said.

"Wait. What are you saying? Are you bi or queer?" I asked.

"I don't like labels."

"What does that mean?"

"It means I don't like labels. My labels aren't anyone's business." She shrugged. "I dated a woman pretty seriously in college before I was introduced to Andrew." Her sad smile shifted into a rueful one and I wondered what memory slipped into the forefront of her mind.

"I can respect that. I don't like them much either." I was afraid to ask, but she seemed to be in a talkative mood, so I jumped in. "Have you dated anyone since…well, since the accident?"

"No."

I don't know why I said it, but the words flew out before I could clamp my mouth shut. I leaned forward and looked at her. "Go out on a date with me. Just something casual. We can ride bikes and get ice cream down at Sharkee's Parlor or drive inland and catch a movie at that small theatre in Pryde's Point." Her face remained passive as she stared back at me. I calmly persisted. "Why don't you think about it and text me tomorrow?" I sat back and folded my hands on my lap as though I didn't just ask one of my favorite artists, my mentor, and a very sexy woman to go out with me. My hands were sweating, and my stomach quivered in anticipation, but I sat as still as possible and waited for her answer.

"I need to go." She stood suddenly.

My heart dropped. I knew it was a long shot, but I had to try. "Okay." I didn't feel comfortable pushing more so I backed down. "Let me walk you home. It's dark out there." Truthfully, I didn't want to stop talking to her. We'd made so much progress over the last few weeks.

"I don't need you to escort me. I'll be fine." She touched my arm and quickly pulled away. It was a habit of hers that seemed to indicate a yes when she didn't want to say it out loud. I didn't mind the closeness, I just hated that she pulled away too quickly. I wanted to give her permission to touch me, but I didn't know how to put it in words. She was too delicate.

"It's no problem. I could use some fresh air and I'm awake now." I grabbed my phone and glanced at the time. It was almost three in the morning. I held up the flashlight I kept by the studio door. "See? A wise woman told me to have one handy because it's not safe out there without light."

Olivia gave a small laugh. "A wise, old woman."

"If you're referring to yourself, you aren't old, but very wise." I closed the door behind us and turned on the flashlight. The crescent moon above afforded us little light, and lingering clouds from the recent thunderstorm blocked any reflection off the water. It was dark.

She clucked at me. "Such a charmer."

"And I'm not even trying," I said. I pretended that the last five minutes didn't happen and walked with her over the small dunes to her house. Her kitchen light was on, but the rest of the house was dark. "Safe and sound." I bowed and pointed at her door. When I turned to leave after saying good night, I felt her hand brush my waist. I turned back around.

"How about Friday?"

I froze. "Date night?" It was the only thing on my mind. I cringed thinking maybe she meant the next tutorial. Her brow arched and she put her hands on her hips.

"Casual get-together." She nodded as though that was an acceptable replacement for the word date.

I pointed at her and repeated. "Casual get-together sounds great." I kept the squeals of excitement inside and retreated into the dark.

"I'll text you later in the week," she said. Her voice got louder the further I slipped into the night. She wanted to be heard.

"Sounds amazing," I said.

We could talk about lessons at dinner. I figured a day or two off from me was exactly what she needed to process any new feelings tumbling around inside her head and heart. This was a massive moment in my life. The rumblings of another fast-moving storm approaching couldn't put me in a bad mood. I had a date. She might have called it something softer, but it involved the two of us going out with the possibility of it turning romantic. I reminded myself to tread lightly because she was so vulnerable. I was also a new person in her life who didn't know what she went through, who didn't see her fall apart, but knew the courage it must have taken to build herself back up. I jumped into her life on the way back to living and I was going to do everything I could to remind her it was okay to open herself up again.

CHAPTER TEN

"Thanks for driving. Again." I fully intended to drive, but I couldn't allow Olivia in my car. I spent an hour deodorizing it, but the carpet cleaner only briefly disguised the smell. Now the inside smelled like musty wet dog who rolled in lilacs. It was so bad that I had to keep the windows rolled down until the carpet and cloth seats fully dried. I was praying it wouldn't rain anytime soon. I was also embarrassed for her to see it.

We were on our way to Pryde's Point for dinner and a movie. We'd picked a romantic comedy that had been out for a few months. It didn't have the best ratings, but I didn't care. Spending time with Olivia was the only thing I wanted.

"No problem. I love driving." Her eyes wandered to the hem of my dress that rested mid-thigh. A slow smile spread across her mouth, and I desperately wanted to know what she was thinking.

I paid rush shipping for a short summer dress I bought online at Nordstrom's end of the summer sale even though it was still July. The hour I spent in front of the mirror fixing my hair and makeup was totally worth it. I couldn't remember the last time I took this long to get ready for a date. Her scrutiny made me feel sexy.

I couldn't tell much about Olivia's outfit on the drive and it wasn't until we parked and she slid out of the car that I could appreciate it fully. She looked incredible. She wore a black sleeveless top and white pants that hugged her form nicely. Her black wedges gave her enough height to where she could almost look me in the eyes.

We continued our discussion about music as we walked into the restaurant. We had discussed Taylor Swift's latest album the entire drive after her current single came on and Olivia tried to change the channel. I'd been too busy trying to explain Taylor's importance to the queer community to ask Olivia about her day.

"How was work?" I asked after we were seated.

"I sold two paintings so it was great."

I reached across the table and squeezed her hands. "Wow. Congratulations. That's wonderful." I wasn't sure how many paintings a gallery on the cape sold in a month, but judging from her reaction, two in a day was awesome. It was a little noisy in the restaurant, but I wasn't letting that deter me from enjoying the evening. I was on a date.

"One was my own."

"That's even better news!"

"So, tonight is my treat because we're celebrating," she said.

I lifted an eyebrow. "At some point, you're going to have to let me buy you dinner. I know I don't make as much money as you do." I paused and smiled because our financial gap was the size of a black hole. "But this date was my idea."

"How about one night you treat us to pizza when we're having a lesson?"

I lifted my hands a tiny bit and did a small cheer that only she could see. "Yay to more lessons. And you're on." Pizza sounded normal, fun, and cheap. And that meant there would be more dates in our future.

"Okay, now you tell me about your day. What did you do?" she asked. Her lips curved against the wine glass as she took a sip of the zinfandel the waiter suggested after we ordered.

"I've been working on a portrait for the Ashfords." The family commissioned me to do a portrait of their three-year-old granddaughter.

"Oh, are you painting Rowan?" she asked. I nodded. "Have you been able to get an idea of her personality? How is it going?"

"Yeah, I think so. I Zoomed with them for a few minutes just to get an idea of what she's like. Caroline also emailed me dozens of photos," I said. Doing Noah's portrait for fun was a lot easier than earning a commission and stressing about it. Olivia's lessons had been invaluable so far. I would have been lost without her advice. "And I think it's coming along nicely, but I would love any suggestions you might have for me. I want to make sure my first commissioned piece is as perfect as possible."

"I'm sure it's wonderful. She's adorable." With similar dark hair and dark eyes, I wondered if Rowan reminded Olivia of Miranda.

"You've met her before?" I asked.

"They've been to the gallery. The Ashfords have purchased a few pieces."

"I'm sure it's super fun and totally stress-free to have a toddler in the gallery." We both laughed.

"Robert held her the whole time. She was sleepy and quiet," Olivia said.

"I'm sure my kids will be complete chaos," I said. Olivia shot me a weird look. "I mean, I just know what I was like growing up. My parents had their hands full. I can't imagine my kids would be any different."

Olivia cleared her throat. "Oh? How many kids do you want?" she asked.

"I'm not even sure I want them. But if me and my partner decide to have kids, it would have to be at least two." It dawned on me that Olivia only had one but that didn't mean she didn't want more.

"Why?"

I recognized I needed to change the subject or else this date was going to die before it even got started. "I grew up alone. I always wanted a sister or a brother to have as my shadow. What about you? Do you have any siblings?"

She nodded. "I have a younger brother, but we don't really talk. Sometimes having a sibling isn't the greatest thing."

I winced. "I'm sorry you don't have a relationship with him. What's the issue?"

She gave me a long look and took another sip of wine. "There's not a specific issue. He just has different priorities than me. He's living his own life somewhere in San Diego in a house my parents bought him. They coddle him even though he's a capable grown ass man with a very expensive degree that he doesn't use."

I cringed thinking about my student loans. I was hesitant to ask. "What's he doing then?"

"He's been writing a novel for five years now. And surfing. And partying. He can't seem to grow up. And he's the baby so my parents cater to him."

"Sounds charming," I said.

She laughed. "That's the problem. He's too charming." She sat up, leaned her elbows on the table, and rested her chin on her hands. "There you go again. Tearing down my walls."

"Is that a bad thing?" I gave her my sexiest smile. She was opening up and the transformation was beautiful. I loved everything about her honesty in this moment.

"I've been running from everyone, but the minute you show up, I can't stop talking," she said.

I barely heard her words because I was concentrating so hard on her mouth. I wanted to kiss those full and inviting lips. "That's not entirely true. It took me a bit to get through, but I knew I wanted to," I said. The air between us felt thick with my heavy words. I needed to lighten the mood. "I'm glad we're out tonight. I haven't given myself some time off in weeks. And I'm pretty sure you've been working constantly this summer." She was at the beach every night but that wasn't necessarily relaxing. "What was the last fun thing you did?"

"Teaching the class. I really enjoy it."

Her smiles always hit me in different places. Sometimes the playful ones did loops in my stomach. The ones that hinted at more depth and meaning hit me right in the heart. It was hard not to think about her past around her, but she was more than her past. "Speaking from experience, you're a great teacher. I know, because I've had several."

"Tell me what you plan to do with your art degree."

I sat back in my chair and blew out a deep breath. "I have no idea. In my head, I was going to make it as an artist, get my work shown in famous galleries, but really, I'll probably wait tables somewhere. I'm pretty good at graphic design. Maybe I'll apply to some corporations. They're always looking." I didn't want to talk about me. I was boring. My future was bleak and I was already stressed enough. "What were your plans when you graduated?" I smacked my palm against my forehead. "What am I even saying? You were commissioned to do the huge mural in the Natural History Museum while you were still in school. I bet you've never looked back."

"I've been very fortunate, but it helps when your family has money. And you get commissioned to do several things over the course of your college career." She sounded confident, not cocky and I appreciated her honesty.

"Grab every opportunity, right?" It was the perfect time for the waiter to return with our dinner. I wanted to get to know Olivia, but I didn't want the whole conversation to be about art. I wanted to know about her. "What do your parents do?"

"Both my parents are doctors."

"Wow. Nice. In Rhode Island or where?"

"New York City. They have their own practice."

"Is that where you grew up?" It was nice learning about her life and her history before her art career. I found out she'd never worked outside the art industry and moved to Boston when she met her husband. "Do you ever talk to your ex-girlfriend?" I couldn't believe I'd waited this long to ask about her. She shook her head. "Not even on social media?"

"I'm not on any social media platforms. I have my website, the gallery site, and that's it. So far, it's worked for me."

I already knew that but I was curious because so much business was conducted online and social media helped promote businesses.

"Your gallery should at least be on Instagram." I quickly backpedaled. "I mean it might even bring more business to the gallery."

"You're right. I just stopped caring after the accident. I know I've missed a lot and I could do so much for the gallery if I promoted it more."

"The good news is that so many buyers know your work that most of your business is probably repeat or word of mouth. But I bet that if you put items in your gallery on Instagram, you'd sell more. Any exposure is good, and buyers will post and tag the gallery if you had a presence. It could only help." I knew some social media sites automatically showed you memories from the day you started an account. Sometimes those memories were hard. I would bet money that she stopped social media because of the constant reminders of her past.

"I know you're right and I should do something sooner rather than later," she said.

I pushed my plate to the side and leaned forward. "New beginnings. If you want help with Insta, let me know. I can give you a crash course. And Noah loves photography. I mean, I know you can do it since you have a website, but it might be fun to give Noah his first photo credit. This could be a nice project for both of you."

She placed her hand on her heart in mock pain. "He loves photography more than my drawing class?"

"Sadly, yes."

She pouted her lips for a moment, but then smiled. "That's actually a great idea."

"I mean, I know you can do it, but it would give him a massive sense of responsibility. He's trying to talk Brook and Cassie into letting him get a dog and they're not budging. He's doing everything he can to show them he's responsible and up for the job. It's an ongoing thing." Anyone could point and shoot, but some of the iPhone shots Noah showed me were amazing. He learned so much in his photography class. I hadn't seen the photos he'd taken with his DSLR yet, but I bet they were even more amazing.

"We should probably go. Our movie starts in twenty minutes," Olivia said. She paid the check and as we weaved our way through the restaurant, I put my hand on her waist as a large party entered the restaurant. I thought she would walk faster, or pause, but instead she reached back and held my hand. I expected her to drop it when we cleared the group, but she held it until we reached the car. I waited for an embarrassed and completely unwarranted apology or an explanation on why she held my hand for a solid thirty seconds, but all I got was a shy smile as she slipped inside the car.

CHAPTER ELEVEN

I couldn't tell you what the movie was about or if we got butter on the popcorn, but I could tell you that Olivia was wearing Birch & Black Pepper Jo Malone cologne. I wanted the connection that we had outside, holding hands while walking to the car. It was simple and sweet and I had been waiting for a breakthrough with Olivia for weeks.

When it was apparent that neither of us was going to eat the popcorn between us, I moved it, leaned closer, and held my hand out. She slid her fingers down my palm and interlocked her fingers with mine. It was simple and sexy and it took half the movie for my heart to settle to a normal pace. I was giddy. When was the last time I held hands with somebody?

"What did you think of the movie?" Olivia asked me on our way back to Goda. It was almost midnight. The bright beams of her coupe sliced the darkness ahead. The soft jazz that we settled on after the Taylor Swift debate played through her expensive sound system. I was sweating even though the air conditioner was set to seventy-two degrees. I adjusted one of the air vents to blow on me.

"Honestly? I don't remember much about it."

"Oh?"

My head was leaning back against the headrest, and I turned to face her. "I was too distracted by my date to pay the movie any attention."

"I thought we weren't calling it a date," she said.

"Time with you. I was too distracted by time with you to focus on anything else."

"Oh." She could've said anything. Either to push me away or pull me in, but she left it in the air.

I wasn't going to push it. I was going to overthink the next fifteen minutes until we pulled into her garage and then I was either going to run or make a move. Even though Olivia's edges were icy, I felt her heat. I knew the reasons she put up walls, I just hoped I knew how to get through.

Instead of driving me to my place, she stopped short and pulled into her driveway. The whir of the garage door opening sounded so loud in the quiet space between us. She didn't move after she turned off the car and we sat there in silence.

"You know, I could—" I never got the rest of the sentence out.

Her hand slipped to the back of my neck and pulled me to her. Our lips met immediately, and I didn't hesitate. I didn't know how long this would last so I was taking full advantage of what she was offering. Her lips were soft and when I pulled her bottom lip into my mouth and gently sucked, she whimpered. I cupped her face with my hands and slowly dipped my tongue inside, tasting her warmth and feeling her tongue gently stroke mine. Never in my life had I wanted to be pressed up against somebody so badly, but the gear shift and the armrest were in the way. I wanted to growl out my frustration. She pulled away first. I slowly dropped my hands.

"This was a very nice not-a-date date." I ran my fingertip down her cheek. "I knew your lips would be incredible." I ran my thumb over them and licked my lips, ready to taste her again.

"I had a nice time tonight," she said.

I couldn't keep my hands off her. I tucked her hair behind her ear and brushed my lips against hers. "So did I." I tried to do the right thing by pulling away. "I should go. It's late and I know you have a full day tomorrow." Saturdays were the busiest at the galleries as people from Boston and neighboring towns flooded the cape. We got out of the car and I met her at the door that led into the house. "Do you want me to go around the front?"

"I should've dropped you off at your place. I don't know what I was thinking," she said. I knew what she was thinking. She wanted to kiss me and wanted to do it in the privacy of her place.

"It's okay. It's a gorgeous night and I could use some cooling off." I locked her fingers with mine and walked slowly to the back door. "I'll swing by the gallery tomorrow and see how you're doing. Maybe I can bring you lunch."

"Text me first. Maybe there will be a lull."

I pulled her into my arms for a hug. I knew this was a big night for her and I didn't want to make her uncomfortable by pushing too hard. I cupped her face again and kissed her softly. "Sleep well. Thank you for tonight." I hated the emptiness I felt after she dropped my hand and opened the door.

"Good night, Josie."

I walked back with a ginormous smile on my face. I wanted to skip but the sand was restrictive, and I didn't know if Olivia was watching me. Besides, the flashlight on my phone wasn't great and I didn't want to fall. I punched in the code to let myself into my place and leaned against the door. What an amazing night.

I jumped in the shower to get the sand off my feet and slipped into boxers and a tank top. I wasn't going to sleep anytime soon.

I grabbed my phone and scrolled through social media, but I couldn't keep my mind from wandering to my evening with Olivia.

Are you still awake?

I almost dropped my phone when I saw Olivia's text.

Why are you still awake? I shot her a message back and settled under the covers expecting a cute exchange until she drifted off to sleep.

Open the door please. I held my phone with both hands as I stared at her message, waiting for my brain to process the words. That meant she was here, right? I jumped up and scrambled to the back door.

"You're here," I said. Olivia stood in my doorway wearing lounge pants and an oversized long-sleeved shirt. Her hair was loosely pulled back and her face free of makeup. She looked lovely. I paused. "Is everything okay?"

"May I come in?"

I stepped aside. "Of course. Come in."

She slipped off her shoes and turned to me. "I think our night ended too early."

I looked at the clock. "But it's almost one. And you have to work tomorrow."

"The gallery doesn't open until eleven," she said.

I wasn't getting it. Her vulnerability and the wisp of clothing that covered her made me want to find a robe and walk her back. It never occurred to me that she wanted me, that she wanted more than just soft kisses tonight.

"I want to be here," she said. She stepped closer. "With you."

Once her words sank in, instinct took over. I pulled her into my arms and met her kiss with wild abandon. We stumbled back to my bedroom. I was afraid to break contact in case this was a dream.

"Are you sure about this?" I had the hem of her shirt in my fingers ready to rid her of it, ready to feel her warm body against mine, but I wanted her to say the word.

She put her hands on mine and lifted her shirt off. "Yes." Her voice was a whisper, but that one word was powerful. It was powerful enough to make my knees weak.

I pulled her on top of me when we hit the mattress and moaned when she spread my legs apart with her knees. It was hot and sexy and I couldn't believe it was happening. Her lips were on my body while her hands pushed my tank up over my head. My adrenaline was a race car pushing my heartbeat to an alarming speed, but even the threat of my heart bursting couldn't stop me. Her wet, warm tongue twirled over my skin and her teeth scraped my sensitive breasts. I wanted to touch her everywhere, but I also wanted her to explore me at her pace.

"How is this happening?"

She stopped. Fuck. Did I say that out loud?

"Do you want me to stop?" she asked. Her voice was throaty and sexy, and her breath was hot on my stomach as she waited for my answer.

"Oh, my God. No. Don't stop." I put my hand over my eyes in embarrassment. "I'm sorry. I didn't realize I used my outside voice." I gasped when her lips continued their journey down my body.

Olivia was not afraid to do what she wanted. Her palms felt hot against my thighs as she pushed them even further apart. When I felt her tongue explore my wet slit, I almost bucked at the sensation. I wrapped my hands in her hair and tried hard not to move my hips into her mouth because it felt amazing. I couldn't remember the last time I had sex and honestly didn't want to. I was here in the moment but trying to stay out of my head at what this all meant. I focused on her mouth and her swirling tongue pressing against my clit. My knees started to shake, and if I didn't stop her now, I knew I was going to come after two minutes.

"Wait. Just a moment," I said.

Her head popped up. "Am I doing something wrong?"

I pulled her up my body so we were face-to-face. "Oh, my God. No." I pushed her hair back from her face. "I just didn't want to come so quickly."

Hearing her soft laughter in the darkness made me smile. I kissed her supple lips, softened by the last several minutes of licking and sucking my sensitive body parts. The desire to please her overtook me and I not-so-gently rolled her on her back and firmly pressed between her legs.

"As fabulous as I think your silky soft lounge pants are, we're going to have to take them off," I said.

She lifted her hips eager to be rid of them, too. My heart almost stopped when I found she wasn't wearing anything underneath. I dropped her pants on the floor and ran my hands up her toned legs until they met at her sweet, wet center. I placed tiny kisses on her thighs and worked my way back up to her face. I was obsessed with her mouth. Her lips were soft and hungry and it took zero time for us to find a rhythm. I stroked her swollen slit while I kissed her mouth and the sensitive spot on her neck. She arched her back when I entered her and moaned in my ear. It was the sexiest sound I'd ever heard.

She ran both hands down my arm and pressed her fingers into my hand. "Faster, Josie."

I felt weak at her command yet determined to give Olivia everything she wanted. She was wet and tight and her smooth walls inside quivered around my finger. I swallowed her deep, appreciative moan. I added a second finger and waited a few seconds for her to adjust to my hand. She moved her hands up to my shoulders and spread her legs. She rolled her hips against my hand and I used my entire body to move against her. My shoulder ached and I shifted my weight to one side so I could fuck her faster and harder. She dug her short nails into my back the closer she was to orgasming. Her entire body was tense against mine, but I wasn't going to stop until I gave her release. Sweat trickled from my temples and my knees were starting to slip on the sheets. I couldn't remember a time when I was only about pleasing the person I was with. Her breathing became more labored and her nails moved from my back to the sheets.

"Yes, yes." Even though her voice was a whisper in my ear, the words boomed inside my head. She rocked her hips into my hand. When she tensed and shouted, I held her tightly until her body stopped shaking and grew limp in my arms. I felt her smile against my shoulder. "That was a surprise."

I looked at her. "But a good one, right?" Did I push her too far? I held my breath while I waited for her response.

She nodded and ran her fingers over my collarbone. Even though it was dark, the thin, bluish moonlight filtered through the partially opened wooden slats and I could see her face and watch the expressions that played across her features. I understood this was a big moment for her. I knew I was the first person she had sex with since her husband.

"You're such a beautiful person even though you try really hard to be an ice queen. Guess what? It's not working," I said. I lifted my eyebrow and kissed her swiftly.

She laughed. "I'm not trying to be an ice queen."

I moved to the side so that my body wasn't smashing hers. "I remember walking into your gallery and you were all snooty and—"

"Snooty? I'm never snooty." She laughed and it was delightful. I wanted to hear it over and over.

"Listen to your voice. Right there! Total snoot. Anyway, before I was so rudely interrupted." I paused to kiss the top of her nose. "You were all dismissive like oh, she doesn't know anything about art." I stopped myself from saying things like I was too poor or too young. This was such a carefree moment and I didn't want to ruin it by bringing up things that we already argued about.

"Okay, maybe I didn't give you a proper chance." She touched my face and ran her fingers over my lips. I surprised her by capturing her forefinger and sucking it into my mouth. Her body twitched when I pulled away.

While keeping eye contact, I moved down her body until my lips were a breath above her clit. "Are you too sensitive?" I darted my tongue over her clit in a quick lick. She moaned. "I'm going to take that as a no."

I spread her lips apart with my hands and ran my tongue up and down her slit. More twitching. When I captured her clit in my mouth, she writhed underneath me. I lessened the pressure until her hips started moving against my face. I held her thighs down and continued sucking and flicking her clit with my tongue until she had another explosive orgasm. She came beautifully. Her body fluttered against mine. A film of perspiration glistened on her stomach and thighs. She smelled like sex and sunscreen. I laid my head against her thigh and ran my hand over her stomach and the underside of her breasts. She was smooth and soft and touching her was very relaxing. I was tired emotionally and physically. I felt her fingers in my hair and sighed at how peaceful I was in this moment. I don't know who fell asleep first or if she even slept at all, but I woke up to her hands touching my body. I was asleep on my stomach and lifted my hips when I felt her fingers graze my pussy.

"Are you awake?"

I moaned. "Yes." I sounded breathless so I said it again. "Yes."

"Yes what?"

Was I supposed to say ma'am, mistress, Olivia, babe? I was too foggy from sleep and too revved up because her hands were on my body. "Yes, please." It was all I could think of in the moment.

She scraped her teeth on my earlobe. "Yes, please, what?"

Now I was fully awake. "Yes, please, fuck me, Olivia."

She pressed her body against mine and slipped two fingers inside when she realized I was awake. I grabbed the headboard and squeezed my pillow. She sucked on my neck and rocked against me. Her strong fingers made me feel weak. I gave up control and embraced the orgasm while the pillow suppressed my screams. It was a fantastic orgasm.

"Wake me up like that anytime," I said.

She practically purred in my ear and snuggled closer. It was the perfect date and even though things happened faster than normal, I think we both realized our time together was limited. The summer was racing by and it was just a matter of weeks before I left this sanctuary of the perfect career, the perfect environment, and the perfect woman.

CHAPTER TWELVE

It was hard not to stare at her when I walked into the gallery. There were several patrons in the small space, but I didn't want to leave. Sometime before dawn, Olivia sneaked out of my bed. I vaguely remember her leaving but I was so exhausted that I couldn't remember if I told her to have a good day. Parts of my body were tender when I stretched awake and sadness washed over me when I realized she wasn't next to me.

"Welcome to Monteclair Gallery," she said. She looked beautiful and I swear she glowed.

I felt like I was floating. This incredible woman, whom I admired for years, and I had the most amazing night together. I wanted to slide up next to her, pull her flush against me, and kiss her slightly swollen lips, but now wasn't the time. I squeezed her hand to have a physical connection.

"Thank you. It looks like you have quite the crowd."

She pulled away first but her fingers lingered on my forearm. "A typical Saturday on the cape."

"Would you like me to bring you lunch? I don't think you'll be leaving anytime soon. Unless you want me to step in for you."

"Thank you, but I ate a late breakfast. I'll be fine until dinner." She wore a blue sleeveless shell and cream-colored pants. Her hair fell in waves down her back. I remembered how it brushed across my skin as she made her way down my body several times throughout the night.

"You look beautiful." The words spilled from my lips before I had a chance to hold them back. She quickly looked around to see who might have overheard and took a step back. I mouthed "I'm sorry" and directed my attention elsewhere when a patron waved her over with questions about a sculpture.

I liked Olivia's gallery. It wasn't cluttered. Each piece had its own space. When it became apparent that she wasn't going to break free anytime soon, I decided to bail. Standing around made me look desperate and I wanted to support her, not stifle her. I waved good-bye when I caught her attention and smiled when she tilted her head and lifted her eyebrow at me. I would see her later for sure. I picked up a flyer on my way out about the end-of-the-summer art fair. I qualified, but I only had a few paintings I could display. I saw Beth through Goda Gallery's window and decided to pop over to say hello.

"Josie. Hi." Beth greeted me warmly. I told myself I was going to have to be a better friend. In the last two weeks, I'd barely even texted her. She pointed to the flyer in my hand. "Oh, are you going to do that? Do you want to exhibit your art here?" I knew she genuinely wanted to help me, but I was unsure of Olivia's plans.

"I don't know. I just picked it up from Olivia's. Since I'm taking private lessons, she might get first dibs."

Beth laughed. "It's really about the artist and giving them the opportunity to be seen. If you're a new artist which you are, then you get one hundred percent commission. It's just our way of encouraging artists to keep creating beautiful things—and it's a good opportunity for the galleries to stay connected to fresh artists. It doesn't matter where your art is, just as long as you get the exposure you deserve." She pointed to the line that said exactly what she just explained to me. Flames of embarrassment flickered on my face.

"I haven't really had a chance to look it over." I glanced around the gallery. It wasn't as busy as Olivia's but Beth had another employee on the floor helping.

"It's almost time for my break. Do you want to go across the street and grab a cup of coffee or an iced tea? Their hibiscus tea is amazing hot or cold. I can tell you more about this." She pointed to the flyer.

"That sounds great," I said.

She smiled warmly. "Let me tell Harli I'm leaving for half an hour. I'll be right back."

As I waited, I looked at the white walls and highly polished wooden floors. Goda Gallery was nice, but it was hard not to compare this one to Olivia's. The space here was a bit cluttered. In my opinion, there were too many pieces on the wall. I liked how Olivia allowed her displays to breathe. How each one had its own space. I slipped outside the gallery to wait for Beth and ran into Noah. His freshly cut hair gave him a more mature look and honestly, it broke my heart.

"Hey, kiddo. How are you?" I handed him the flyer. "Are you going to do this?"

"Definitely. So far, I have five prints each of four photos. They're all matted and ready to go. My instructor helped me pick them out and showed me how to number them. I'm sure I'll add more."

"That's so cool. Save me the number one print of your favorite photo. That way when you become rich and famous, I can tell the world that I have a Noah Wellington first print."

"Okay, I know the one. I'll save it for you." He beamed with excitement. I knew photography was going to be his thing.

His new camera was top of the line, and he was spending all of his time learning its functions. He tried to explain some of the buttons to me when he first got it, but my eyes glazed over and I nodded repeatedly until he wandered off to take photos on the beach.

I high-fived him. "Awesome. What's going on today? Are you hanging with your friends?"

He shrugged and the tiny blue embroidered whale on his white T-shirt barely moved. "We're going snorkeling by the house later. Then play some games. Maybe you can jump on tonight?" Last week, I played *Minecraft* with Noah and Hayden. A storm had rolled through preventing me from going out on the beach and I didn't feel like painting. Three hours came and went in a flash.

"I don't know. I have to finish two paintings."

"For the fair?"

"Actually, no. I was hired to make them," I said.

"That's so cool. I can't wait until I can make money doing what I love."

I remembered the conversation Olivia and I had last night about hiring Noah to take the gallery photos, but it wasn't my place to say anything in case she was only humoring me.

"I'm sure it'll happen soon enough. It's the best feeling in the world. Where are you headed?"

He pointed to the blue and red store with a bright sign illuminating the name Sun Comics. It was the only place besides Cape Beer that had neon. "I'm going to check to see if they have anything new."

"Have fun."

He gave me a little head nod and crossed the street.

A minute later, Beth joined me on the sidewalk. "I'm ready." She closed the door behind her and followed me across the street.

Beth and I had already grabbed coffee a few times and I was thankful I'd met her. I knew that she worked at Goda Gallery from April until November and lived in a small one-bedroom apartment above the gallery. She moved inland to her family's estate during winter where she passed the time reading, visiting New York City to shop, and writing her family's memoir. Her family was wealthy, but not as wealthy as the Wellingtons. Apparently, their history before the nineteenth century was riddled with scandalous moments and she was all about exposing them. It sounded interesting and I told her that once she published it, I wanted a signed copy.

I ordered a hot tea and grabbed us seats that overlooked Ocean View Drive. It was too pedestrian-packed to drive on the weekends so this was a primo spot to people-watch.

"I'm so glad to get out of there for a bit. I don't know why people try to haggle. Weekends are tough," Beth said.

"Who's Harli?"

"They're my cousin. They'll be graduating college soon so next year we'll have to hire somebody new."

"A family business. That's cool," I said.

"What do your parents do? Do they support you as an artist?"

"Both of my parents work for other people. Nobody knows where I got my artistic talent from." My dad was content working for H&R Block as an accountant and my mom worked part-time at the local animal shelter. They were never going to be rich, but they loved what they did. When was the last time I checked in with them? Two weeks after I got here? "Let's just say I'm going to be paying off my student loans until I'm well into my thirties. They love that I have talent, but they don't see how I can make a living doing this." If I didn't have commissioned work rolling in, I would've left here feeling very discouraged. I owed everything to the Wellingtons.

"How many paintings do you think you can exhibit? You still have time," Beth said. I mentally counted the ones I had done and that were good enough for the world to see.

"Maybe a dozen?" For sure I wanted Olivia's input. And honestly, I wanted all of mine to be at her gallery. "What usually happens during the event? How big is it?" Beth's eyes lit up and she sat up straighter in her high back chair.

"It's huge. Goda shuts the street down. We put up tents in case the weather is dicey and have panels of artwork for several blocks. Local vendors set up food. There's live music. It's just such a fun day."

I looked over the details on the flyer again. "It sounds like a lot of fun." And a lot of stress. "Do you need help setting up?"

She waved me off. "Oh, no. Thank you. We have plenty of hired help." She looked at her watch. "I have to get back to work in a few minutes. What are your plans the rest of the day?"

I was hoping she didn't want to go out later because I was saving the evening for Olivia. "I'm going back to the house to look for a job. I'm going to have to get back to reality soon."

"Any prospects?"

I grimaced because the thought of leaving this place was tortuous. "Honestly? I haven't even started looking. I'm in a fairy tale and I don't want it to end."

She put her hand on my arm. "That's what makes this place so wonderful. It's so laid-back and it's as if the rest of the world doesn't matter," she said.

She was right. I couldn't remember the last time I looked at the news. I didn't care about the local events. Beth kept me updated on things in town I might like even though I hadn't done a single thing she suggested except grab a burger and a beer with her one night. My driving force was time with Olivia.

"I'll never forget it, that's for sure," I said.

Beth looked at me quizzically. "I mean, you'll be back, right?"

I snorted. "Maybe when I start making money. It's kind of expensive." Beth didn't struggle like I did.

"I get that. Well, just know that I hope you come back. Even though Goda is already special, you've made it fun."

"Thank you. I'll come back to visit for sure. Even if it's just for the day," I said.

Beth looked at her watch and pointed to the gallery. "Time's up. Thanks for the tea and the company." She recycled her cup and gave me a hug. "I'll see you later. Think about what I said about displaying your work during the fair." She wagged her finger back and forth between her gallery and Olivia's.

"Will do. See you soon."

As alluring as going back to Monteclair Gallery seemed, I decided the best thing to do was go back to my place, spend about an hour looking at jobs, and paint. If tonight was going to be a repeat of last night, I was going to need the time I was apart from Olivia to finish my projects. I picked up a lobster roll from a walk-up window and made my way back to Revere Estates. I was either going to be in the food industry or entry level at a graphic design company. I'd make more money waiting tables, but I was hoping to doing something remotely related to my degree. Either way, I would be scraping.

I sent my résumé to four graphic design companies in Boston and two in Providence. One of my instructors at RISD said she knew a company in New York who would hire me in an instant, but did I want to live there? My future was fuzzy, and I could feel myself shutting down because it was all too much to think about right now. I closed my computer and headed to the studio. Painting was a great stress reliever. I could get lost in my work and forget about the pressures of my unknown future.

❖

Are you busy?

I wiped my hands on my smock as I read Olivia's message. It was seven. I'd been painting for five hours. It was therapeutic and had been a full two minutes since I thought about her. *Just painting. How are you?* I decided I was done and my night belonged to whatever Olivia wanted to do.

Long day. I just got home about ten minutes ago.

It took you this long to text me? I followed it up with a wink emoji. *Have you eaten yet?*

No. I just put on comfy clothes.

Oh? Like last night comfy clothes? God, my texts were annoying even to me. One wink emoji per conversation was enough. I needed to cut my emoji usage by half. I bit my lip as I waited for her response.

Ha ha. Sort of.

Would you like some company? I can whip up something for us to eat. I was a horrible cook but I knew how to make a tasty omelet. Olivia struck me as somebody who always had fresh vegetables and a stocked refrigerator. I wondered if she had an assistant or a housekeeper. I never saw anyone, but that didn't mean there wasn't somebody around. Olivia had a big house. It wasn't as large as Revere Estates, but it was several thousand square feet.

Let's cook together. Come on over. I'll get started.

I quickly showered and put on shorts and a long-sleeved T-shirt. I didn't bother with shoes since the path from my place to hers was nothing but sand. "Hi," I said breathlessly when she opened the back door.

"Hi." She stood back and allowed me to enter.

I ran my fingertips across her stomach when I walked by. I could smell food and looked at her. "I don't think you waited for me. What are you making?"

She closed the door and leaned against it. I didn't hesitate. I moved into her space. I interlocked my fingers with hers and I slid her hands up the door until they were above her head. The move brought my body flush against hers. Her gaze traveled from my mouth to my eyes and back down to my mouth. She wanted me to kiss her. I smirked and obliged. I'd been thinking about kissing her again since I woke up. I wasn't gentle and neither was she. Her mouth was hot and her tongue dipped inside my mouth, stroking until I moaned and my knees grew weak. She broke the kiss.

"Shit, the food," she said.

I let her go and waited for my wobbly legs to work again before I followed her. In twenty-four hours, this woman had turned me to mush. Every part of me grew soft when she was near including my heart, and that was not a good thing. I didn't need an emotional entanglement with my life so unsettled.

"Since you didn't wait for me, what did you fix?" I walked into the kitchen with my nose in the air trying to figure out what she was making. "Something with garlic and shrimp."

"I'm making shrimp scampi."

"That's your 'I'm-going-to-throw-something-together' meal?" I asked. My omelet seemed so simple and not at all impressive. "It smells wonderful." I watched as she stirred the pasta in with the sauce and shrimp and expertly split it in half over two plates. "It looks so much better than what I was going to cook. Know now that I am not a great chef."

She rinsed out the pan and left it in the sink. "Lucky for you, I am. Grab your plate. Would you like to sit out on the deck?" She poured us glasses of wine and headed out the patio door. The sun had already set, but it was still a gorgeous evening and not too cool.

"It's so beautiful here." I sat next to her so we could watch the fading light together. Even though we were inches apart, I knew emotionally she was in a different world. I remained quiet but aware of her.

"Another reason I hate moving back to the city," she said.

"So, you'll be here until December. What happens to the town? Do most people only visit during the summer?"

"Some places stay open. That's why I know so many people and restaurants. There are only a fraction of businesses and people who operate year-round," she said.

"And here I thought it was just your natural charisma." I winked and smiled because even though it felt like I was teasing her, I meant every word.

Olivia lifted her brow and smirked. "Anyway, enough about that. Tell me about your day. What did you do?"

I swallowed hard. I didn't want to have this conversation right now. "I sent my résumé to half a dozen graphic design businesses." When she took a sip of wine, I saw her hand shake ever so slightly. "Four in Boston and two in Providence."

"Any I know?" she asked. I listed them off and she nodded at Loquist and Meyers, the two firms in Providence. "You can't go wrong with either one of those." She showed zero reaction when I mentioned the ones in Boston. Ice queen was back. Or at least some of the walls were back in place. Apparently, talking about moving to or working in Boston was off-limits.

"I'll figure out where I'm going to live once I land a job." Graphic design wasn't my ideal career path, but I needed to get my name out there before I could live off commissions alone. The Wellingtons had given me such a massive boost, but it would still take time to build a customer base.

"There are some places outside Providence where the rent isn't horrible. Boston is pretty high. You'll probably need a roommate or two." She cringed as though she felt sorry for me.

"I wish the summer would never end." It was the most honest thing I could say without giving too much away. "Why can't I live and work here forever? I could paint portraits and seascapes and take walks on the beach. Oh, I know why. Because this is a fantasy and reality sucks."

A sad smile slid across her face. "You'll find something that you'll enjoy." She took a sip of wine. "This summer has been…" she paused. I mentally crossed my fingers wanting her to say something meaningful. "Fun. It's been fun," she said. Not the word I was looking for, but it certainly let me know where she was coming from and that we weren't in the same place.

"Definitely fun." I tamped down any emotions that would disturb the delicacy of this moment. I changed the subject. "This is delicious, by the way. Just something you threw together, huh?"

"I hope it's not too garlicky. I always overdo it."

"It's perfect." We ate in companionable silence. I kept thinking about last night. It was everything I imagined and more. I wanted to express my feelings, but I got the feeling that Olivia wasn't exactly that kind of person. She was extremely private even though we did some extremely personal things in the bedroom. "It's not too late to go for a walk," I said.

"I'd like to go sit by the water if you don't mind," she said.

I helped her up and we moved closer to the beach. We sat in the moonlight and listened to the waves gently slide over the sand. The water was calm tonight.

"Miranda used to beg me to come out after bedtime," Olivia said. I became very still because she didn't talk about her daughter often. "She wanted to see mermaids who rode seahorses and starfish who tumbled out of the sea and ran on the beach. She said they could only come out at night because it was too dangerous for them to be seen by humans. She had the best imagination." The smile on her face took my breath away. It was pure and beautiful and exemplified what I thought was true love.

"Tell me more about her," I said.

Olivia picked up a handful of sand and let it drift between her fingers. "We built sandcastles all the time. Her goal was to see how high she could build one before the ocean washed it away. And she was never mad when it did. It was a game to her." The love in her voice was evident. "She had a tremendous seashell collection and was great at finding whole shells and sand dollars. The kid was born for the beach."

"She loved it here."

Olivia nodded. "She really did. That's why I can never sell this place. It's home."

"Do you have to leave in the off-season? Do you have to go back to Boston?"

"It's hard to go back and forth, especially in the winter. The weather is treacherous and it just takes too long to go inland for supplies. And it's easier to procure art in the city and ship it out from there. Plus, Boston at Christmastime is wonderful," she said.

"Getting snowed in here is probably magical," I said. I'd never been on a beach during the winter. I hated the cold but could probably tolerate it, especially in a house like hers. I wanted to go back inside because I wanted to touch her again, but she was so at peace here under the vast sky and twinkling stars. I finished my wine and lay on the beach with my hands under my head while she told me stories of her family and what she was like as a kid. I saw a shooting star and wondered if it was her daughter tumbling like a starfish against the dark sky—happy and carefree like the stories she told her mother.

CHAPTER THIRTEEN

*H*ow's *work? Do you need anything? Lunch? A quick visit?* I asked.

If you're offering...

Oh? Are you hungry? I was ready to run to whatever restaurant Olivia wanted.

It would be nice to see you.

It was hard not to read into it. Maybe something great happened at the gallery. Maybe she sold more paintings, or maybe she just wanted to see me. *Do you want any food?*

No thanks. See you soon.

For somebody who was going to walk away from me at the end of the summer, she was sending me mixed signals. I slipped into one of my few summer dresses and took about twenty minutes to freshen up and try to look my best without looking like I was trying so hard. I jumped into my car and was at the gallery in minutes.

"What took you so long?" she asked. She looked amazing. I loved it when she wore her hair down. Her black suit skirt was tight and I took a moment to appreciate her form as I strolled up to her.

"Red is definitely your power color," I said.

She blushed and looked down at her blouse for a moment before making eye contact. "Thank you. I don't wear it enough, but I should."

Three nights ago, she wore a red lacy bra and panty set and dominated me in the bedroom. Every time I saw red now, I thought about how she straddled me and told me exactly where to put my hands, where to touch her, when not to touch her, and where my mouth could go. It was the hottest sex I'd ever had. Not just because she was sexy as hell, but because she was very controlling and took her time. I looked around. There was only one patron in the gallery and it was only a matter of time before he left.

"It makes you very bold," I said.

She raised an eyebrow and scraped her teeth on her bottom lip. It was obvious she was thinking the same thing. We slowly walked around, talking about art we'd already talked about until the patron exited the gallery. She pulled me behind the wall and away from the front door.

"How's this for bold?" Her arms snaked around my waist as she stepped into my personal space and kissed me passionately. I cupped her face and pressed her up against the wall. The painting next to us swayed. I slowed down only because this wasn't the place for hot and heavy.

"Bold is nice, but so is soft and sweet." I kissed her softly and it changed the whole dynamic of the moment. I felt her tremble in my arms as I moved my mouth from hers and made a soft trail of kisses down her neck, along her jaw, and back up to her lips. "Hi." She ran her fingertips over my mouth as though studying them.

"Hi."

"Did I scare off a potential buyer by loitering?" I pulled both of her hands around my waist so she was embracing me. She smiled and locked her fingers just below my hips.

"Not at all. He was just looking."

I playfully peeked my head around the wall. "Was he looking at you? Do I need to have a talk with him?" I made my voice stern and pretended to be jealous.

"Not at me. He's been in before. He can't seem to pull the trigger on the Tutu painting." She moved one hand to cup the back of my neck and bring my lips down to hers. Her mouth was warm and she tasted like mint.

"Mm. I'm glad you wanted to see me." I was kidding myself that I wasn't going to read too much into it. We'd had incredible sex but only a few tender moments. Every time things hinted at a more emotional level, Olivia would change the subject or shut me up by kissing me. This was a nice change.

"The gallery is surprisingly slow today. Any luck on the job front?" she asked.

I sneered and put my forehead against hers. "A few nibbles. Hopefully, something will pop soon. I did get asked if I was available to Zoom next week but we didn't set a date or time." I knew I interviewed well. I wasn't an extrovert, but I knew what people wanted to hear. Interviewing was easy. Accepting and changing the course of my life was hard.

"I'm sure something will happen soon," she said. I liked the way her eyes roamed my body. "You look really cute today. That's such a good color on you."

I looked at my teal-colored dress quickly brushing my lips over hers. "Thank you. I probably should've packed more clothes, but it was far more important to bring all my art supplies."

"You know that if you need anything, my studio is available to you."

"Thank you. So far, I'm doing okay, but I will take you up on your offer if that changes." I felt her fingertips inch up my dress. My eyes widened in mock shock.

"Olivia Monteclair, what are you doing? We're in public. Anyone could walk in or see us through the window."

She played innocent. "I don't know what you're talking about." Her fingers fluttered lower. "I just wanted to see you again." We literally spent the night together. She saw me less than twelve hours ago. Even if she pretended this was only about sex, I knew this was more.

"I have an idea. How do you feel about being on the water?"

She gave me a quick peck and moved her hands from around my waist up to circle my neck. The tiny hairs under her fingers stood up as chills marched their way slowly up and down my body.

"Like what exactly?" she asked.

"I would love to go out on the water with you for one of our casual get-togethers." I stopped calling them dates because she acted differently every time I said the word. "Maybe a dinner cruise or a whale watching tour. Just something different, but I don't know if you get seasick or don't like that kind of touristy stuff." In all honesty, I wasn't sure if being in the ocean was tough for her because of her family. I tried to sound casual, but I was worried that my date idea would be a trigger.

"I haven't done a whale watching tour in forever. That sounds like fun."

I almost lifted her up because I was so excited that we were going to be out in public and not keeping our relationship only in the privacy of her house and my bedroom. "Awesome. How about tonight? I think the weather is supposed to be calm. I can run down and get us tickets." It was also a way for me to pay for a date. I didn't have to pay for pizza last night because they were so late delivering it that they gave it to us for free. It was my goal to pay for something sometime before I left for the summer.

"I think that sounds great. I think the last tour is at six. I can close down early, run home and change my clothes and then pick you up by five thirty."

"That sounds like a plan," I said. I pulled her flush against me and kissed her until we were both breathless. We broke apart when the bell chimed as somebody entered the gallery.

"I'll be right there." Olivia smoothed down her skirt and gave me a quick, sexy smile before disappearing in front of the wall. I heard her greet two customers before I emerged and walked by them.

"I'll see you later, Olivia." I gave her a swift wink before leaving her to plan our casual get-together. Regardless of what we did in public, in my heart I knew that we would end the night in her bed.

❖

It was a beautiful, calm evening. I managed to get tickets on a semi-private boat which promised a close encounter with animals in the ocean.

Olivia grabbed a blanket from the tiny trunk of her car and held it up as though to prove a point. "We're going to need this."

"Really?" I fanned my T-shirt from my body just to catch a breeze. It was hot and I was starting to sweat.

"You didn't take my advice and wear jeans so I'm improvising," she said.

"But I remembered sunglasses." I still had her glasses from the night of the Wellingtons' summer kickoff party. I pulled them down an inch to look her up and down. I wagged my eyebrows at her and gave a low whistle. "You in jeans…" I gave her an okay symbol. She looked amazing. The sleeves of her black linen shirt were rolled to her elbow and the jeans hugged her body perfectly. I pointed to her loafers. "Those don't look water safe." They looked fashionable and expensive.

"Worst-case scenario, I'll go barefoot. Come on. I want to get a seat up front." It was precious to see her so excited about something as simple as a whale watching tour.

We found two seats in the front and accepted flutes of champagne from the same guy who took our tickets. There were four other couples, a family of four, and a mother and daughter duo with heavy camera equipment slung around their necks. My iPhone with the cracked screen was going to have to do. Noah would've had a blast taking photos.

"Hey, how's Noah doing? I'm so glad Brook and Cassie agreed to let him photograph your gallery's art," I said. I bet he would have a dog by Christmas.

"He's very good. We're getting a lot of traffic on Instagram. Cassie tweeting and tagging us on her Instagram hasn't hurt one bit either," she said.

I laughed. "Yes, I know firsthand how important it is having the Wellingtons as friends. Think about how much my life has changed this summer. I mean look at the connections I've made." Olivia gave me a weird smile and cleared her throat. Great. I made her uncomfortable. "Do you want something else to drink? I don't really like champagne." I slipped away from the sudden awkwardness and found a small bar at the end of the boat that offered soda, bottled water, and wine. I asked for two waters and grabbed a bag of pretzels.

"Everyone take your seat," the captain said. "We're pushing off in a minute. We've received word from a boat that's heading back to the harbor that there is a pod of whales a few miles south so hopefully we can catch them."

I made my way back to Olivia. She acted as if nothing had happened and thanked me for the water. "Can you believe a pod of whales? How cool!" I said. Even though I lived relatively close to beaches, whale and dolphin watching was never on my radar. Plus, I never had disposable income before. Not that I could afford tickets like these whenever I wanted, but sometimes it was okay. I wanted to do something special for Olivia, but not make it obvious.

I leaned against the railing and lifted my face to the sun. I smiled when I felt her hand rest on my leg. Goda was queer friendly, but this was the first time she touched me openly in public. Granted, she didn't know anybody on the boat, but it was a big step in my eyes. This made it more than just a secret fling.

She leaned closer so I could hear her. "Thank you for this. It's nice to get away."

I held her hand because it felt natural and I wanted the connection. "Are you as excited to see baby whales as I am?"

"I'm just excited to be out on the water again," she said. I didn't ask because deep down I knew the last time was probably with her family.

"It's the perfect day. Calm weather, beautiful woman, lots of sea creatures."

She turned and the look on her face almost prompted me to caress her cheek. We'd had zero conversations about the future, but the way she looked at me in this moment told me there could be one.

"Dolphins!" Somebody in front of us pointed at the water, breaking our moment.

We both turned and looked over the railing. "Oh, my goodness. Look at how many!" I grabbed my phone and snapped several photos. It occurred to me that I didn't have any photos of Olivia. "Hey, let's take a selfie with the dolphins behind us." I scooted closer and held my phone up. "Ready?" I snapped one of us before remembering to take my sunglasses off. Olivia followed my lead and took hers off as well. I took about ten photos hoping at least one turned out. The reflection of the lowering sun was bright on the water so I was shooting blind.

"We're coming up on the pod. Please stay in your seat and look at the bow or the front of the ship. I see four or five whales up ahead." The captain pointed forward to the people who couldn't figure out where to look.

I tried to pretend that it wasn't a big deal, but inside I was squealing. "Look! There's the mama and baby."

Everyone scrambled over to our side of the boat much to the captain's chagrin. "People, you need to stay seated or use the handrails to move around. We don't need or want any of you to fall overboard." There was surrender in his voice as people from the other side moved to our side.

I pulled Olivia closer to me. She leaned against me as we watched several whales swim close to the boat. I slid my phone in my pocket and kept my arms around her instead. She was the magical part of this moment. Yes, it was incredible to see majestic sea life right in front of us, but I could always go on a whale watching tour, just not with Olivia.

"This is incredible," I whispered. I folded my arms around her shoulders when she leaned into me. Even though she always changed the subject when I brushed the topic of the future, I knew she felt something for me that wasn't just lust. It was hard not to think or want more.

"I haven't seen a baby and mama whale in years," she said.

"I haven't seen this many dolphins or porpoises ever in my life." For being a kid from the East Coast, my family didn't spend a lot of time at the beach. We all took it for granted and only went when there was a party or family reunion. By the time the captain turned the boat around, the sun was setting and a cool breeze followed us back to Goda. Olivia spread the blanket across our shoulders. It was long enough to cover our laps, too. "You were right."

She shrugged. "Beach life. Always prepared for the unexpected."

Olivia ran her hand lightly up and down my thigh under the blanket. At first, I thought it was just something comforting until she moved her fingers closer to the apex of my thighs. I darted my eyes around the boat to see if anyone was interested in us or could even see movement under the blanket.

"What are you doing?" I asked, knowing full well what she was doing but questioning her timing.

She pulled her hand away slowly and chuckled. "I was playing around." She kissed my cheek and the corner of my mouth.

"Keep the thought and all those feelings for about thirty minutes." I could see the harbor off in the distance and knew it would take about twenty minutes to dock. "I really like casual get-together night."

"I do, too." She looked away as though something striking off in the distance caught her eye, but not before I saw a little slip and a swirl of emotions in her eyes. Tonight, was going to be tender and special. I could tell her guard was already down and when that happened, we made love slowly, passionately, and communicated with our hands and our lips. "I have a surprise at home."

"Will I like it?" I asked. Her surprises were always top notch. Me asking the question was just humoring her. I more than liked them. I loved them. The devilish smile told me that I would and it was going to be awesome. "Are you going to give me a hint?'

She pursed her lips and pretended to be deep in thought. "Okay. You wear it."

I hoped it wasn't lingerie because that wasn't my thing. I loved her matching bra and panty sets, but she knew I didn't wear things like that. The only thing I wore were boxers and tank tops. I sat up straight. The only thing that crossed my mind was a strap-on, but she wouldn't know what to get or what I was comfortable with. "Wait. Did you get it on your lunch hour?"

"No, before work."

My clit twitched and I pulled the hem of my shorts away from my throbbing center. "Did you get it down the street from the gallery?" Goda's Goddess of Love was about half a mile away. I always joked about going there, but she never once indicated she was interested.

"You'll find out later."

"Hmm." I didn't want to get my hopes up because there were T-shirt stores and gifts shops that sold socks and sweatshirts. For all I knew, she got me a Goda sweatshirt. "Sounds great." I pushed my sunglasses back on my head to keep my hair from blowing into my face and ignored her expressions because I didn't want to get all worked up for nothing. "I'm going to shower before we eat if you don't mind. My hair feels salty and I'm pretty sure I have sand in places I shouldn't."

"Did you go down to the beach today?" she asked.

"I did after I saw Beth from Goda Gallery. We talked for a bit on her lunch break." I felt Olivia stiffen next to me. Was she jealous of Beth? I knew that our relationship wasn't strong enough for me to tease her about it, so I ignored her reaction. "She's the first gallery I visited when I arrived. Her boyfriend is coming up this weekend so she was telling me everything they had planned." I felt her relax after I said boyfriend. I didn't tell Olivia I got the idea of the whale tour from Beth. "Do you know her well? She seems pretty cool."

"We're competition but she's very nice. Wilford Aston owns the gallery and he's a massive jerk. I always avoid him when he comes to town. I think he's Beth's great-uncle," she said.

"Where does he live?"

"Worcester. The gallery is more of a hobby for him. Beth has done a remarkable job of bringing in clients despite her poisonous uncle."

"Wow. You really like him, huh?" I teased her.

"He tried to get my husband to invest with him, but Andrew didn't like the way he did business and Wilford wasn't happy he was turned down. A part of me thinks he opened the business next door just to spite me."

"How long as it been there?" I asked. I pulled the blanket off us and folded it as the crew secured the boat to the dock. Olivia recycled our bottles and reached for my hand as though we were a couple and this was normal behavior. I swallowed hard and pulled her closer to me in case she stumbled on the ramp off the dock.

"Three years ago."

"Fuck him. What a dirtbag." I quickly looked around hoping the family with kids wasn't behind me and heard.

She tightened her grip on my hand. "He came up to me at the funeral and said he would be more than happy to help me with my finances and wouldn't charge me full commission."

My mouth dropped open. "Yeah, I get why you hate him. And here I thought this was paradise."

"When he's in town, I lock my house." She tossed the blanket in the trunk and slipped into the car. I was still processing the information. Why did Beth work for such a douchebag?

"I hope so. Has he ever just dropped in?"

She pulled into slow traffic and waved at a couple crossing the street. "He stopped coming by after I told his wife that I wasn't interested in doing business with him since one of Andrew's partners handled our finances. I also told her that it made me uncomfortable when he dropped by without an invitation."

"That's ballsy and I love it." I couldn't imagine saying something like that, but then I'd never had a creeper and this guy sounded dirty. "Do you have an alarm system?"

She shrugged. "Like I said before, we've never really had an issue with people breaking into homes before. Every summer there are cars that get broken into, but that's pretty normal for a beach town. Unfortunately, the chief of police plays golf with Wilford."

"You need some protection. You're out here all by yourself and I don't like that at all."

Olivia smiled and touched my face. "Don't worry. I've taken care of myself this long. Besides, Brook and Cassie are two houses down if I need help."

I was stressing out. She needed a bat or a mean watchdog or something that would give her time to get away if there was an intruder.

"How is Cuddles with other animals? Like a Rottweiler. Hey, maybe you and the Wellingtons can get litter mate German Shepherd or Akita pups at a shelter somewhere. That way they can grow up together and you both will have protection." I didn't point out that the Wellingtons left in September, leaving Olivia alone for months.

"A dog in Boston sounds horrible. There isn't any grass where I live," she said. I didn't realize she had pulled up next to my house until she pointed at my door. "Why don't you get ready and come over in about an hour. I'm going to need to shower, too."

I slipped out of the car and walked over to her side. "Lock your door from now on. I'll knock on the back door in sixty minutes."

She ran her fingertip along the neckline of my shirt. I felt a slight tug as she playfully looked down the vee her finger created and smirked. "Hmm. It's sweet that you're so worried about me, but I'm a fighter and I know where all the knives are in my house." She winked and slowly backed down the driveway.

I shook my head and punched in the code to the house. The wind had picked up, and according to my weather app, a storm was approaching but wouldn't hit us until midnight. My plan was to stay the night because I couldn't imagine Olivia kicking me out or driving me home at two in the morning. It was getting harder to leave our get-togethers and I hoped she felt the same.

CHAPTER FOURTEEN

I was early. It was a struggle not to show up even earlier. Olivia had already showered and was almost done making dinner. "It's amazing what you can do in an hour," I said.

"It's only pasta. That doesn't take any time at all," she said.

"You're amazing. This is too much." I walked around the kitchen island and put my arms around her waist while she stirred some pesto on the stove. Fresh vegetables were roasting in the oven and a bottle of wine was open and breathing on the counter next to two wine glasses.

She turned so that we were facing one another. I kissed her softly. Her damp hair was loosely braided and hung over one shoulder. She was wearing a soft black T-shirt that was tight across her breasts and black pajama shorts. She wasn't wearing a bra and her nipples strained against the material, but I knew she did that on purpose.

Everything about tonight screamed sex. The energy in the room made my heart pick up pace and my body hum with excitement. I was going to take my time with her tonight. I ran my fingertip down her neck and over one of her breasts. She closed her eyes as I brushed my hand over the fullness but didn't cup it.

I tilted her chin up. "You're so beautiful, Olivia." I placed a soft kiss on her lips and moved away when the timer dinged. Her hands shook as she opened the oven to flip the vegetables over. "Is there anything I can do?"

"Maybe pour us some ice water. Dinner should be ready in about seven minutes."

"What could we do in seven minutes?" I asked. I shot her my most innocent look and bit my bottom lip before raising my eyebrows.

In a move that surprised me, she sat on the counter and pointed to the wine bottle. "We could toast to a good day." She picked up one of the glasses and held it up to the light as though she saw a spot on the crystal. She carefully put it back down and pushed both glasses away from her. "We could talk about the weather. There's a sixty percent chance that the storm will hit us after midnight tonight." She slowly spread her legs and made sure I was watching. I was mesmerized. "Or we could make out until the timer goes off." She said it casually and leaned back on the palms of her hands so that her hips were right at the edge of the counter.

We were probably down to six minutes, and while I knew that was enough time to make her come, I wanted tonight to be different. There was a shift happening. It felt like our relationship was at a turning point. I walked over to her and put my hands on her knees and spread her further apart. I fucking loved how limber she was.

"Making out sounds fun, but I'd hate to get interrupted." I leaned back and looked at the timer. "We have five minutes and forty-one seconds. I want more time. Once I start, I'm not stopping and I don't want this food to burn."

She gave a short laugh. "So, you're saying the food is more important than me?"

I wrapped her legs around my waist. "Not at all. But eating will give us energy and I'm going to need a lot of carbs for tonight."

"Oh?"

I kissed her soundly. "I saw the bag by the front door." I pushed my hips into her and moaned when she did. "I'm almost certain you got me a strap-on to fuck you with and if I'm right, I'm going to fuck you all night long and well into the morning." I watched her reaction to my words. Her eyes narrowed with want. I pressed my hand between her legs and moaned when I felt how wet she was. "And if I'm wrong and you didn't buy me that, I'm going to need the car and a hammer so I can break into Goddess of Love and find the perfect dildo for us."

"Fuck," she hissed between clenched teeth.

I grabbed her ass and brought her against me. She pulled at my clothes, and as much as I wanted to fuck her in the kitchen, I wanted her first orgasm of the night to come from the dildo. "Lean back," I said.

She let go of me and leaned back on her palms again. I ran my hand up one leg of her shorts until I felt the smooth, wet skin of her pussy. I inhaled sharply, loving the smell and feel of her. She leaned back on her elbows so that her hips tilted up. I glanced at the timer. Three minutes fifteen seconds. I could still make her come. I brushed my fingertips up and down her slit. She pressed against me when I touched her swollen clit.

"Yes, Josie."

I wanted to rip her shorts off and lick her until she came, but I had a plan. I lightly tapped her clit until she squirmed for more pressure. "Am I right? Is that what you got me to wear?"

"Yes." Her voice was low and raspy.

"Do you really want to come right now or do you want to wait until we can go upstairs? What sounds better? I know what I'd like."

She sighed deeply. "You're right." She started to sit up, but I put my hand gently on her chest and stopped her.

"I didn't say we weren't going to make out in the two minutes left. I just didn't want you to come." I watched her face as I slipped two fingers inside her. Her eyes fluttered shut and she moaned loudly. Just one thrust made her legs tremble. I slipped my hand under her shirt and cupped her breast. I rubbed my thumb and forefinger across her rock-hard nipple and squeezed the same time I thrusted my fingers inside her again. Her legs trembled harder. "I'm going to do that two more times and then we have to stop because I can tell you're getting ready to come." Her nostrils flared but she nodded. "I want to be on top of you and inside you and feel your body move underneath me. You understand, right?" There were thirty seconds left on the timer. I thrust twice and pulled out before she came. My knees felt weak and I was lightheaded. I watched as her breathing slowed and kissed her when she leaned up.

"I'm going to eat really fast," she said. She let out a strained laugh and straightened out her clothes.

"I'm not. I'm going to eat slowly and taste everything."

She swallowed hard and slid down the cabinet when the timer shrilled that dinner was ready. I didn't think I had it in me to tease, but fuck, not only did it work, Olivia was totally into it.

❖

I was surprised at the size she picked but also loved the strap-on harness she chose. It was snug and gave me a lot of control. I took several deep breaths before throwing on the soft, white bathrobe that she left on the back of the door. I walked into the bedroom. She had turned off the lights, but opened the curtains so moonlight spilled into the room, cascading across the bed. I stopped and held my hand over my chest.

"Did I scare you again?" Olivia asked.

"No, you took my breath away."

She was naked on the bed with the covers pulled back. Her hair cascaded across the pillow and every feeling I had about our relationship came rushing forward. "Take off your robe. I want to see my present."

I slowly untied the sash. "But I thought this was my present."

She leaned up on her knees and pushed the robe off my body. I felt her fingertips brush my thighs as she admired her purchase. "Let's call it ours. Now get into bed."

I crawled under the covers and reached for her. What started as an extremely sexually charged moment changed the minute she slid into my embrace. She was softer and the mood shifted into something gentler. She kissed me and pressed her body against mine. I ran my hands up her back and held her close. I settled into the moment and stopped trying to figure out what to do next. I felt strong feelings tap in an unfamiliar way against my chest. When she rolled off me, I followed until I was resting between her legs. I could feel her hips gently push into mine seeking friction from the dildo that brushed against her slit. She moaned every time I stiffened and the tip of the dildo pressed harder against her.

"Just like that, Josie."

Her words empowered me. I grabbed the lube from the nightstand and leaned back on my haunches to apply it. The way she watched me work it up and down the shaft kickstarted my heart and made my clit swell. There was hunger in her gaze, but something else. She was completely unguarded. Maybe she thought the moonlight wouldn't show her emotions in the darkened room, but I saw them.

"Are you sure about this?" I asked.

She answered by pulling my face down to hers and kissing me. She bent her knees and lifted her hips letting the dildo drag up and down. I reached down for better control of the strap-on and teased her. She moaned her frustration and kissed me so hard that her teeth pressed against my bottom lip, cutting it. I pulled back to run my tongue over the small injury.

She rubbed her thumb over my lip. "Are you okay?"

I nodded and sucked her thumb into my mouth. She pulled her hand away to bring my mouth down to hers. This time she was slow and gentle and it was the perfect moment to slip into her. I leaned up on my elbow and used my free hand to guide the dildo down her slit and carefully push. She dug her nails in my back and moaned. I almost pulled out, thinking I was hurting her, but she wrapped her legs around my waist and lifted her hips until I was all the way inside. She arched her back and cried out.

I stilled my body to keep from coming as the base slammed into my clit. It was my turn to ask. "Are you okay?"

Her breathing was labored but she mumbled something breathless and nodded. She was ready. I slowly moved my hips, thankful for the snug fit. My face was even with hers. I looked into her eyes with every slow thrust and watched as her eyes narrowed the deeper I got.

"Let go of my waist," I said. Once she obliged, I was able to move my hips faster. She writhed beneath me, but never broke eye contact except when her eyelids fluttered shut at the pleasure she was feeling. I pulled out all the way and smiled at the confused look. When I pushed back into her, she moaned.

"Oh, that's nice. That's really nice," she said.

I did it again. All the way in, and all the way out. Her body was tense. Sweat beaded up on her face, neck, and stomach. I could feel her body quiver beneath mine. As much as I wanted to explode into an orgasm with her since she was so close, I decided to drag it out a little bit longer. I pulled out and whispered in her ear, "Roll over."

Olivia didn't hesitate. She flipped over and lifted her hips in the air, waiting for me to enter her. There was something so carefree and perfect about this moment. I ran my tongue down her sweaty back, nipped a trail over her ass, and licked her wet, swollen core. I pushed her hips down to the mattress and climbed on top of her. I slid inside of her carefully because I knew the angle was different and the dildo she picked was large. I scraped my teeth along the tight muscle on her shoulder.

She pressed her palms into her pillow and arched her back. "This is perfect. You're…" She stopped and I strained to listen. I wanted everything from her tonight. Her approval, her lust, her devotion, and her heart.

"I'm what?"

She bit her lip and grasped for the headboard. "You're… you're perfect." It was almost a whisper but I heard it. There was no way she was using me for sex. Even though she was hell bent on avoiding discussions about what we were, in this moment, I knew we were more.

I rewarded her honesty with a brilliant orgasm while riding one out of my own. I would never forget how trusting she was of me. Her walls were down, her beautiful body glistened with sweat, and the sweet smell of sex was everywhere. I gently pulled out and rolled off her. Her body rose and fell with every deep breath she took. I drew patterns with my fingertips along her back until she shivered, rolled over, and curled up next to me. I pulled the blanket up over us and held her close.

Lightning danced and burned across the sky as the storm rolled in. Olivia snuggled closer when thunder loudly followed the flickering brightness. I didn't care. I was exactly where I needed to be.

CHAPTER FIFTEEN

Thanks for talking to me. I appreciate the advice." I was sitting on the Wellingtons' deck drinking a cup of coffee with Cassie. The coffee was stronger than I liked, but I didn't complain. I wrapped my fingers around the mug finding comfort in the heat and the sharp aroma. Ava was down for a quick, morning nap, Brook was back in Boston for a board meeting, and Noah was at a friend's house for an overnight. If anybody could relate to what I was going through, it was Cassie. "So, how long did it take you to win over Brook?"

Cassie laughed. "She fought the attraction for months. She said we were on different paths and I wasn't ready for real love because I was so much younger than she."

I dropped my head in my hands. "This sounds so familiar. I don't know how to get through to Olivia that I don't care about our age difference." Olivia and I had been together physically for almost three weeks. Twenty days of either mind-blowing sex or soft cuddles on the couch. It was hard not to develop feelings when you knew every inch of somebody and had seen the joy and pain in their heart.

Cassie patted my hand. "You all have a lot more than just the age difference. While I think it's great that Olivia opened up to you, her situation is very delicate. I know you know that, but you have to be very careful with her."

"I really like her. I came here to improve my craft and expand my portfolio. In the process, I found somebody I admire who helps me be a better artist and I'm falling for her. I'm really living the dream." I saw the knowing smile on Cassie's face. "Just like you are." I knew I didn't have the right to tell anyone about my clandestine relationship with Olivia, but I trusted Cassie and I needed to talk through my feelings. I didn't have anyone else.

"I think you should take what she gives you, and who knows? Maybe it'll be more after the summer. It took me about three months before Brook even looked at me as more than just the nanny. Even when she noticed me, she kept me at arm's length. I got weird and confusing signals," Cassie said.

"How did you get past that? What did you do to sort out what was happening?" This was the information I needed to know.

"Eventually, I figured out that she was just trying to push me away because she didn't want to fall for me. I was patient and told her how much I loved her and how we were perfect for each other. It took time for her to really believe me. There are more years between us than between you and Olivia. It hasn't been easy, but we've made it work."

"What's been the most difficult thing in your relationship?" I asked. I quickly added, "If you don't mind talking about it."

"Time. Brook has a very demanding job. We've had several conversations before we decided to have Ava. I needed her home more and I had to cut back my hours, too. Taking care of the kids was the most important thing."

"So, really no age issues?"

Cassie laughed. "I mean, I don't understand some of the movie references she makes. She hasn't watched anything in years, but some of the lines she blurts out are so random. And she refuses to learn social media. I use it for our foundations and charities. She sees the importance of it but knows it can be poison." She leaned forward and whispered, "I've been known to scroll for hours."

"Same." It didn't sound like there was anything major about their age gap and that made me feel better about a future with Olivia. Brook and Cassie were my example.

"And I like to game and she doesn't. She's not interested and I get that. I only play with Noah when she's not home," Cassie said.

"I can't imagine Olivia wanting to play video games. We spend most of our free time walking on the beach and drawing or painting."

Cassie topped off my coffee. "I love that you have that in common. That means you both know what's important for each other and that speaks volumes," she said.

"We spend a lot of time in her studio." I added an extra splash of cream to cut down on the bitterness. It didn't help and I didn't want to insult Cassie, so I sipped it.

"Do you want to know what I think?" she asked. She squeezed my hands. I nodded and squeezed back. Any advice was appreciated. "Even though we have a lot in common, our situations are very different. Brook's walls around her heart seemed impenetrable. I didn't know if I was ever going to get through. She looked through me, around me, over me, but never at me. Her ex-wife really hurt her. She didn't want to feel love again and it took a long time for her to trust me. We were able to overcome our issues with patience and kindness. You can show Olivia patience and kindness all day, every day, but that won't work. Her pain is very different and stems from extreme loss," Cassie said. She slid off her sunglasses and topped off her coffee cup. I waved her off when she offered me more.

"I don't know how to help her get past that," I said.

"Olivia needs proof that you're not going to be taken away from her and that's not something you can do. You can't guarantee that something won't happen to you. Nobody can. She needs unwavering presence, but she's not willing to open herself up and give you the chance. That doesn't mean she won't. It just means you can't force it."

My shoulders slumped. Cassie was right. Olivia was going to continue to push me away until I didn't have a choice but to leave. I wasn't going to win and that crushed me. "Every time I try to talk about a possible relationship outside of Goda, she changes the subject."

Cassie nodded. "It's going to be a battle. I know how stubborn Olivia can be. You'll just have to enjoy the time you have left and see what happens in the fall. Speaking of, have you found a job yet?"

From the six résumés I sent out, I had two Zoom meetings scheduled after passing phone interviews. My portfolio was strong enough that I wasn't worried about getting a job, I was worried about where it would be. Ideally, I would have loved an internship to work with an artist, but that never paid, and I didn't have the funds to cover expenses for a year. Not to mention the student loan payments I would have to start in a few months. I had to settle for a career in graphic design. My only question was should I focus on the Boston area and keep trying to have a relationship with Olivia or go for the best job for me?

"I have a Zoom call in a bit and one on Friday," I said.

"Are you excited about them? Is that what you want to do?"

I shrugged. "I'd prefer to just paint, of course. And I like graphic design, but starting at the bottom is hard. There isn't a lot of freedom when you design for customers. They have an idea of what they want and sometimes it's hard to give them what they see in their minds." The summer between my junior and senior year, I interned at Global Awareness in their marketing department. A lot of my designs weren't used because I was too "artsy." It gave me tons of hours, but very little creative credit. I checked the time and realized my Zoom interview was coming up and I still needed to get ready. "I've got to prep for my interview. Thanks for talking to me, Cassie. I really appreciate it."

"I'm here if you need me for anything," she said. "And let me know if you need advice on Ava's portrait."

I hadn't shown her anything yet and decided to wait until I was completely done. I loved Noah's portrait, but I thought Ava's was better. Olivia suggested that I add similar colors so the portraits matched. I knew they were going to love it. I wasn't as meticulous on Rowan's portrait, but it was still good and worth the price tag, according to Brook. I wasn't comfortable asking for such an exorbitant amount. It was mind-blowing to me still.

"I should be done with it by the weekend." I was taking my time to get it perfect since they were paying me.

"No hints? Not even a peek?" she asked. I shook my head. "How about I stand at the studio window and you flip it around for a second?"

"Nope. Not until it's done."

Her nose crinkled adorably and she snapped her fingers. "Darn it. Okay, I can wait. I just love Noah's portrait so much. You're so talented." When we stood, she hugged me. I wasn't expecting it, but I welcomed it.

"Thank you. And thanks again for the advice."

"You're welcome," Cassie said. She leaned over the railing as I walked away. "And if you need help picking paintings to put in the fair, I can come by anytime."

I waved to her as I walked back to the studio. "You're just trying to get a sneak peek."

She shrugged. "Can't blame a girl for trying."

I hoped that I would stay in contact with the Wellingtons after the summer. Not because they would recommend clients to me, but because I genuinely liked them. I wasn't frightened around Brook now and I thought Cassie and I could be genuine friends. Plus, both kids were super cute and happy.

I stood in the middle of my studio with my hands on my hips and looked at the paints and sketches I'd finished. I was pleased with my progress and had over a dozen various sized paintings of the ocean, people strolling through town, crabs and shells on the beach. It was a good display of my summer and the progress of my craft.

Olivia had insisted on displaying most of my art at the festival. I thought it was a conflict of interest, but she said she was my instructor, and she wasn't taking no for an answer. She had favorites and assured me there were buyers already interested in *Morning Starfish*, *Sunset Rival*, and *Conch Shell*. I trusted Olivia to price them. She knew the climate of the town and the visitors. I would scream with joy at fifty dollars a piece, but I had a feeling Olivia's price tag would be more than that. Noting the time, I quickly changed my clothes for my interview. I found a soft peach colored top that made my tan pop, and I threw my hair back in a neat bun. The sun had given it nice light streaks. I looked like I belonged on the beach. I put on a minimal amount of makeup. I was still wearing shorts, but the people I was meeting with wouldn't be able to see what I was wearing from the waist down. I angled the camera and checked my lighting.

Seven minutes before the scheduled Zoom, Olivia texted, *Are you done with your meeting?*

Just sat down. It starts at one.

Oh, I thought it was at noon. Good luck! I'm sure you'll wow them. I am more than happy to be a recommendation if you need one. It never occurred to me to ask her for a reference and it made my heart flutter in a confusing way. Did I want her to help me move away? It was an incredible offer, but it also made me feel more like a student than lover or whatever title she had for me other than girlfriend.

Thank you! If they need one, I'll be sure to give them your name. That's very sweet of you. I threw in a smiley face because she didn't owe me anything.

Call me when you're done. If you want to talk about it.

Thanks. Will do. Signing off for now. I turned my phone on silent and logged into the meeting. While I waited for Meyers Advertising to admit me, I did a quick check of myself and my surroundings. I looked good against the teal walls and bookshelves full of books that looked and smelled new. I sat up straight when my computer blinked and four people appeared in squares on my screen.

"Hello, Josie. It's nice to meet you. I'm Rosaline James and these are my colleagues Jeff White, Preston Jenus, and Emily Taylor." The other three people gave me quick waves.

"It's nice to meet you. Thank you for taking time to meet with me." And the interview was underway. I answered questions about my goals and my future the best I could. After forty-five minutes, they thanked me for my time and said they would get in touch with me soon.

And done! I sent Olivia a text message.

How'd it go?

Okay. They seem like a good company. I didn't get warm fuzzies with them, but they were reputable and had excellent benefits.

I've heard good things about them.

My heart sunk that she gave very little input. We were getting along so well that I just assumed she would be okay with me wanting to get a job close to her. I knew this wasn't a summer fling but maybe she still thought it was.

CHAPTER SIXTEEN

W e're so happy you said yes. I didn't want a summer to go by without having at least dinner." Brook hugged Olivia.

I handed Cassie a bottle of wine. It came from Olivia's private stash so I knew it was expensive. I cradled it on the walk over here afraid I might drop it. Olivia teased me that we were walking on soft, loose sand and the bottle wouldn't break, but I still held it like a tight end with a football getting ready to be tackled.

I was nervous enough. This was the first time we were showing up as a couple in front of people we knew. I had worn a path from the guest house to Olivia's so it was ridiculous for us to pretend that Brook and Cassie didn't see us either on their security cameras or through the windows. Olivia didn't have an alarm system, but the Wellingtons did. I didn't want to think about what they possibly saw; I only hoped Noah didn't have access to the feed.

"I'm so sorry I didn't come over sooner," Olivia said. She smoothed her hair back with the palm of her hand—something I knew she did when she was nervous.

Guilt poked at my conscience. I was the one who kept Olivia from spending time with them. I didn't hear what Brook whispered, but Olivia's cheeks brightened and they both looked at me. I quickly looked away.

"So, Noah's at Hayden's. Where's Ava?" I asked Cassie.

"My sister-in-law is upstairs rocking her to sleep. She'll be down in a minute. You'll like her."

I knew this was a small dinner party because there were only two additional cars parked in the courtyard. I wondered who else was joining us.

I didn't take any chances and wore my little black dress and black sandals. Olivia wore a white sleeveless wide-leg cutout jumpsuit that showed off her tan. We looked incredible together. I wore my hair down, but hers was pulled back in a messy bun that took her about twenty minutes to perfect. At some point in the evening, I predicted that I would pull my hair up into a ponytail or bun, and she would let hers down. Watching her get ready had been such an incredible turn-on.

"I know this isn't a working dinner party, but Erica can't wait to meet you. She loves your work and I'm sure she'll want portraits done of my nieces," Brook said.

"Yes, we all saw the painting you did of Rowan and it turned out amazing. I prefer the ones you did for us, but I know I'm biased," Cassie said.

"Thank you." I wasn't even going to pretend that I wasn't super proud of theirs because I was.

Brook handed me a glass of wine and pointed to the charcuterie board. "Help yourself. I'm going to steal Olivia away for a few minutes. We'll be right back."

Olivia looked pointedly at me and raised an eyebrow before following Brook. I turned to Cassie. "Hopefully she's not in trouble for skipping out on you all summer," I said playfully. Cassie waved me off.

"Oh, no. They go way back. If they don't return by the time Erica gets down here, then we'll go looking for them." Cassie turned her attention to the food in front of us. "I skipped lunch knowing there would be a feast tonight and I'm not afraid to dig in." She handed me a plate before piling different cheeses, meats, dried fruit, and small breads on her plate.

"Nice. I didn't skip lunch and I'm still going to follow your lead." We stood around the large kitchen island and chatted about food while waiting for everyone to show up.

"Lacy, my best friend from college, should be down any minute. It's just the six of us. We're a good mix," Cassie said. She wore light camel-colored ankle pants and a black sleeveless shirt. Her scalloped ballerina flats had delicate designs embroidered on them.

"I'm looking forward to a fun night," I said.

"Erica's a riot and Lacy's humor is very dry. They're both without their children tonight so—" her thought was cut off when someone busted into the room startling both of us.

"Where's the wine? Oh, hi. You must be Josie. I'm Erica." Erica shook my hand and poured herself a glass of wine. "I've heard a lot about you. A lot. Like tons. It's nice to finally meet you." She clinked her glass against mine. "Where's Olivia?"

I pointed behind me. "Brook took her somewhere. Hopefully, they come back soon."

A woman a little bit older than me stumbled into the kitchen wearing lounge pants and an oversized sweatshirt. "Why didn't somebody wake me up sooner? I'm a hot mess."

"You're beautiful, babe." Cassie pulled her into a hug. She straightened the woman's clothes before presenting her to me. "Josie, this is Lacy. Lacy, meet Josie. She's the artist living in the guest house."

"Hi. It's so nice to meet you. Everyone talks about you so much that I feel like I already know you." She rubbed her eyes and stifled a yawn. "Sorry. I'm not trying to be rude. I just got off a thirty-six-hour shift and I'm dragging."

"It's nice to meet everyone." I didn't know what else to say, but I felt myself relax around Erica and Lacy. They seemed down-to-earth and within minutes, our conversation about movies turned into an impromptu guess the movie by the line game. I didn't know how long we'd been playing, but after Cassie poured me a second glass of wine, I started worrying about Olivia. It was as if we were somehow connected because I turned right before she and Brook returned to the kitchen. Her smile made me smile so I knew whatever they talked about didn't upset her.

"Olivia, we're dropping major movie lines. Loser has to drink if they don't know it," Erica said. That wasn't the game at all, but they giggled and I went along with it.

I shrugged. "This is my second glass if that tells you how bad I am."

"You're not on my team then because I will win this game. Are we even playing on teams?" Olivia asked. She gracefully took a glass from Cassie and stood directly across from me. It was hard not to stare. Honestly, every single woman in this room was attractive, but Olivia's sexiness was palpable. And she was mine.

"Let's go sit," Erica said, waving her hand in front of her face to fan herself. "I'm starting to feel this wine and I'd rather be sitting so that I don't make an ass of myself by falling down."

"Let's go, lightweight," Brook said. She hooked her arm around Erica's and walked her to the dining room. We followed with our glasses of wine.

I hung back a few steps until Olivia caught up to me. "Is everything okay?" I whispered.

"It's great. Don't worry." She squeezed my hand and sat next to me at the table. It was going to be hard to keep my hands to myself, but Erica was on the other side of me and I needed to be on my best behavior.

We oohed and ahhed when Chef Patrick delivered hot and cold appetizers. They looked and smelled delicious. We patiently waited until he explained each dish and told us to enjoy. Even though I nervously ate my way through introductions thirty minutes ago, I still had room for more. I was happily munching along until Erica turned to me.

"How long have you two been dating?" I froze and stared straight at Cassie who was directly across from me. She lifted her eyebrows and turned her attention elsewhere. I didn't know how to answer that since Olivia made it clear we weren't dating. I swallowed and took a sip of water. "We're not really dating. We're just kind of enjoying the summer and each other's company." I refused to look at Olivia and prayed I said the right thing.

Erica pursed her lips at me and tilted her head. "Ow…oh?" She disguised a groan with a small cough when a motion under the table made me believe that somebody kicked her. Everyone opposite me looked innocent. She moved her chair back. "Well, you are striking together. Whatever you're not doing, it looks good on you."

"Thank you." I desperately wanted to change the subject and I wasn't above selling myself to do it. "By the way, Brook said you might want portraits of your children." Erica whipped out her phone and showed me pictures of two kids wearing backpacks, standing in front of a house.

"Here they are. First day of school. Griffin is almost ten and Willow is six. I adore the portraits you did of my niece and nephew so I definitely want you to paint my children," she said.

"They're so adorable. Noah speaks so highly of them." Who says that? Noah liked hanging out with them because they liked to game and Griffin always kicked his ass at chess. I loved that at twelve, he was a good sport about losing. Not too many kids were that mature.

"They're ornery, but I love them." She stared at her phone so long that, for a moment, I thought I was off the hook. She lowered her voice and leaned closer. "You all remind me of Cassie and Brook from years ago. I was their biggest cheerleader then and look at them now." I had to say something or else Erica was going to pull Olivia into the conversation. From what I could tell, Brook was having a heavy conversation with Olivia about real estate and thankfully, they weren't paying attention to us. "We're keeping it casual since I'll be leaving in a few weeks."

"Goda has a small airport. You could commute. Long distance isn't really a thing anymore," she said. I didn't know why she was so invested in our relationship. Nobody really knew about us anyway. It was obvious Brook and Cassie had filled her in, but even they didn't know what was happening.

"Well, first thing on my agenda is to get a job. Then everything else will work itself out. I'm not worried." I shrugged like tearing out my heart and leaving it here wasn't a big deal when I knew it was going to be the hardest thing to do. But I couldn't make somebody want to stay with me. It had to be organic, and even though I knew Olivia cared for me, I didn't think it was enough even though being with her was foremost in my head and my heart.

"You're going to kill it. Everything in life. I have a good feeling about you," Erica said. She must have gotten the hint because she switched topics and pulled us into the conversation Cassie and Lacy were having about social media.

"I keep telling Brook social media can be very helpful to businesses. It brings a level of humanity to Fortune 500 companies especially when people see the good that large corporations do. Too many bad things are exposed, but you don't hear about the good very often. Social media helps get the word out," Cassie said. The passion in her voice was unmistakable.

"It's a double-edged sword. It can also spread bad news like wildfire," Lacy said. She stabbed a piece of shrimp and chewed it quickly before continuing. "I see both sides. I get on my phone to get immediate news, see super cute cat videos, and watch politicians implode." She held out her hand and numbered off with her fingers. "It's immediate, it's forever, it's unforgiving, and it's entertaining as hell. It can also be vicious and cruel. I understand why Brook doesn't like it and why she doesn't want Noah on it."

Cassie rolled her eyes. "It's like anything else. You have to ease your kids into it. Like teaching them to ride a bike or drive a car. You have to monitor them, teach them right from wrong, and tell them everything on the internet is forever. And kids will make mistakes."

"That's what I mean. Why even get them started?" Lacy asked.

"So, keep them in a cave and let the world keep turning without their input? It's not feasible to keep them from the internet. Which means we need to give them the right tools and lessons to manage it. I feel like Noah will make good decisions," Cassie said.

I couldn't imagine a life without social media. My whole life had been electronics and the internet. I had my Game Boy with me at all times when I ran errands with my mom. I remember going to my dad's work on in-service days and hiding under his desk to play on Nickelodeon's website on his personal laptop. They had games, videos, and tools to entertain kids for that very situation. My mom had both Myspace and Facebook accounts. I always saw her posting and scrolling.

I couldn't stay silent. "I'm twenty-three. Social media has existed my entire life. I'm not on it that much other than for the same reasons Lacy said, but that's because I'm so used to it. I know not to post stupid things that will haunt me later." Everyone stopped and stared at me. "My profession is very visual so posting on social media is important. I want people to see my art, and it's a great way to build a business fast."

Cassie reached across the table and high-fived me. "Damn right. It's the way of the world now."

I nodded. "It really is. It's something that parents need to talk to their kids about just like anything else that might be a threat. Noah has been doing a remarkable job with Olivia's gallery Instagram. I mean, Olivia writes the words, but Noah understands the concept of why it's important to the gallery and how to choose words wisely," I said. Brook looked at me sharply and I felt like I'd said too much.

"I don't disagree. I just don't like to lose that much time at once. I know how quickly one gets lost scrolling." Brook softly bumped Cassie's elbow.

Cassie laughed and raised her hand. "Hi, my name is Cassie and I have a TikTok problem." I laughed when Erica and Lacy raised their hands, too.

"I want Noah to still be a kid and ride his bike and swim in the ocean and play with friends outside. I know all of this is inevitable. Social media is both good and bad and hopefully our children will make good decisions," Brook said.

Cassie covered Brook's hand with her own. "He's a smart kid and he knows right from wrong. Ava will be trickier, but we have about eight years to prep," Cassie said.

"You're going to have to sign me up for TikTok. Who's going to show me all the cute videos when you're gone?" Olivia asked. Her words stung. We watched TikTok in bed either first thing in the morning or right before falling asleep. We wouldn't have that after Labor Day.

I mustered a smile. "Once you have an account, then I can send you videos."

I focused on the general conversation about social media and the latest trends. It was too hard to think about Olivia's words. We were on a date with new-to-me friends and she acted like it was no big deal. I was positive everyone understood what was happening because they softened toward me. By the time the main course was served, I was full, but I was eating my feelings and kept shoveling food in my mouth. Olivia leaned closer. Her breath on my ear made me shiver.

"Don't eat too much. You don't want to be uncomfortable later," Olivia said right when there was a lull in the conversation. Everyone looked at me. I knew what she meant, and judging from their reaction, so did they.

"I promise that won't be a problem." I blushed as I looked at the few bites I had left on my plate. I pushed them around with my fork before I put it down. Maybe it was the wine, but I was feeling extra clingy. "You look amazing tonight," I said. Her neck flushed delightfully and she looked at me with longing. My heart swelled. Silence blanketed the table as all eyes were on our exchange. Emotions I recognized and some I didn't swirled in the depths of her brown eyes. I didn't look away until Erica cleared her throat.

"Okay, so what crazy things are happening after dinner? I'm afraid I ate too much and drank too little," Erica said.

"Let's go out on the deck. It's a gorgeous night," Cassie said. She stood and waited for us to grab our drinks and follow her. I lingered and stepped in Olivia's path. When we were the only ones in the room, I pulled her in my arms and kissed her. She moaned and gently pulled away when it was obvious I wasn't going to stop.

She put her hand on my arm. "Let's go be good guests and we can finish this when we get home."

I almost smiled at how domestic that sounded. I didn't realize how desperately I wanted to hear her validate our relationship even if it was only in the privacy of us. "Okay. Later." I put my hand on her back and followed her to the group out to the deck.

We went outside and Erica waved me over to help her pick what music to put on. Olivia made a beeline for the bartender. I'd never been one to drink a lot, but this summer Olivia made me a wine aficionado by trying all the different bottles in her cellar. I was afraid to ask how much each bottle was worth so instead I appreciated that Olivia wanted to share the experience with me.

We spent the rest of the evening carrying on a light conversation. Olivia purposely sat away from me. Erica and Lacy danced to cheesy eighties music while the rest of us cheered and rated them. The more they drank, the higher the scores. It was a fun evening, but I wanted it to be over so that Olivia and I could finish what we started in the dining room.

CHAPTER SEVENTEEN

With a week left in Goda, it was time to make a choice. I needed a paycheck and a place to live. Meyers Advertising offered me the best benefits with the most creative freedom. I knew Providence well enough to be able to find a place quickly. I sent my acceptance email and went to the beach. I wasn't going to be back here for a long time, and the sadness I felt was overwhelming.

The art fair was tomorrow and that meant a day of loitering down on the square and trying not to obsess whether my art would sell. I gaped at the price tags Olivia had attached by the canvases. The two that Beth had hanging up in her tent were equally priced.

"You're going to be a name whose art people will want. We have to let them know that they are getting a bargain," Beth said.

If everything of mine sold, I would have a really nice nest egg. My savings account already had a nice chunk from commissioned artwork, which included a hefty payment for Ava's painting. I wouldn't give the Wellingtons a price, so they went overboard and paid me what they thought it was worth. I told them it was too much, but they insisted it was fair. It was plenty of money to get started somewhere. I had a few personal items in a storage locker in Providence that I could get my ex-roommate to help move.

My life was sprinting forward even though I wanted to stay on the beach and in this moment forever. I walked in the wet sand and let the cool water wash over my feet. I loved the sounds of the ocean. It was so calming even when it was roaring before or after a storm. I made a promise to myself that I would take time and visit Newport Beach at least once a month. It was only an hour away from where I was thinking of living.

As much as I would miss the beach, it was time to acknowledge that what I'd really miss was Olivia. The reality of my situation weighed heavily on my mind. Olivia and I needed to have a serious conversation about the future. Was I her rebound or was there something more? Every time I tried to bring up a possible relationship after summer, she changed the subject or stopped me by asking me to help her with something. It was obvious she didn't want to have the talk.

When I approached Revere Estates from the beach, I could see Cassie and Brook sitting on the deck under a giant blue umbrella.

"Josie, come on up. Say hi," Cassie called.

I joined them and thanked Cassie for the glass of lemonade. "I can't possibly thank you enough for this summer. It was unforgettable."

"We loved having you. I heard you found a job. What company did you decide to go with?" Brook asked.

My shrug was involuntary. "Meyers Advertising in Providence. Their graphic design program does more than just computer-generated art so hopefully I'll have the opportunity to showcase some of what I can do."

"I hope that you met a lot of people who will continue to commission your talents. I know Robert loves the portrait and, of course, we love ours as well," Brook said.

They looked like such a happy, peaceful couple. Their age gap wasn't an issue so why was Olivia making it one for us? I wanted our relationship to continue. Providence to Goda was an hour and a half and about the same from Providence to Boston.

"This has been the best summer of my life for so many reasons. I'm excited to start a new chapter, but it's hard to let go of all of this," I said.

"We're happy to be a part of it," Brook said. She surprised me by squeezing my forearm. "I'm sure you'll do wonderful things in your career."

Why was I getting choked up about people I only knew for a few months? It wasn't as if we spent a lot of time together. "Thank you so much." I was doing that thing again where I could hear myself thanking them entirely too much, but I couldn't stop because it came from my heart.

Brook casually flipped back her hair. The day was warm, but she looked cool and collected. "I know you are processing a lot right now, but watching Olivia fall for you reminds me of when I fell for Cassie. I had so much I had to fight through." She threw that dart right at my heart. I wasn't sure what to say. My eyes drifted between them. They were perfect together and seemingly had it all. Brook carefully pushed. "I hope you have the same drive as Cassie. She never gave up."

I sighed and fought hard to keep the tears from falling. "I'm going to respect her wishes and leave things the way she wants. I don't want to seem like a stalker."

"There's nothing wrong with pursuing happiness. Obviously, she makes you very happy and likewise. You're the first person to make such an impact on her since the accident," Brook said.

"It's so nice to see her happy again." Cassie's smile gave me false hope. Just because they recognized what I felt in my heart and what maybe Olivia felt, too, didn't mean anything would happen.

"She's not interested in a relationship." My voice sounded defeated. My heart felt the same. It was like a chunk of granite. They didn't need to hear my whimpering. I cleared my throat. "Thank you both for your support of my art. I hope I'm not out of line, but I consider you my friends."

Cassie squeezed my hand affectionately. "I feel the same way. I'm sorry we didn't spend more time together, but we didn't want to take you away from your passions." She lifted an eyebrow at me and I couldn't help but smile at her obvious innuendo.

"I appreciate that." I laughed a little too hard only because my stored anxiety was finally finding release.

Cassie sobered up first. "If you haven't told her how you feel, I think you'll always regret it." She waved me off when I tried to interrupt. "Don't be scared. Take it from me. If you don't at least have a heart-to-heart, you'll always wonder what if."

Hope ignited inside me like a spark on dry kindling. I stood, determined to go fight for a relationship that I didn't think had life. "You're right. I need to have one serious talk before I leave." I wasn't entirely convinced that we would make headway, but it was worth a shot.

"Good luck," they said in unison.

I knew Olivia wouldn't be home for a few hours so I spent the time cleaning my place. It was the best way to work out every scenario with Olivia in my head. I packed up some of my things that I wouldn't need for the rest of my time and made a small pile by the front door. I checked the time. Olivia would be closing soon. Maybe I could meet her and we could have a quick dinner in town. I changed into shorts and a button-down casual shirt and walked across the warm sand to downtown Goda.

"Hi, you," I said.

Her face lit up when she saw me. "Hey, you." Even if she didn't admit it, she was happy to see me. Her body leaned into my personal space and the smile she gave me hinted at more than just friendship. I saw it and took a step back. She had two customers milling about.

"How's business today?"

"It was busy but productive. I had a Zoom meeting with an artist out of New Jersey. He's agreed to sign with Monteclair. And I just received confirmation that the first two weeks in January, Boston Premiere Gallery will display several of my artists' work."

I wanted to hug her because she looked so happy and stress-free. "Wow. That's amazing news," I said.

"I've contracted with them before, but this is the first one I've been excited about in a long time."

"That's really good progress. I'm proud of you."

Light pink spread across her cheeks, and she lowered her gaze to the floor. I wondered when the last time somebody told her they were proud of her. She waved my praise off. "Thanks. Working with other, larger galleries keeps me busy during the winter months. I might even do something with Schmidt Gallery in New York," she said. When she looked at me, there was a fire in her eyes that I hadn't seen before.

I was equally impressed. "That's really huge," I said.

"They've reached out a few times, but I wasn't ready, you know? I think I'm in a better place now and ready to work with other galleries."

"Sounds like we should celebrate. How about we grab dinner somewhere? My treat," I said.

"Something light. I'm too excited to eat right now." She put her hands on her stomach and let out a deep breath. She was magnificent in her element. I felt proud and weirdly responsible because I got through to her when nobody else did. I checked the time. She still had fifteen minutes before closing. "Want me to come back in fifteen?"

She grabbed her keys off the desk. "I'm going to close up early." She followed the patrons to the front door. "Thank you for coming in." She locked the door and flipped the sign from open to closed.

I gave a small clap. "Excellent. Where would you like to have dinner?"

She surprised me by grabbing my hand and walking me to the back door. "I need to make sure this is locked so I figured we can just leave this way, too. Why don't we just grab salads and head back to my place? Did you walk here?"

I nodded. "I took the shortcut. Plus, it's a nice day for a walk." I looked at her heels. "But not in those shoes."

"You look adorable and different." Her eyebrow quirked a little as if she was confused.

I looked at my outfit even though I knew exactly what I was wearing. The button-down shirt was form-fitting and the shorts hit right above my knee. I bought a pair of navy boat shoes on sale at Beach Feet that matched my shirt. "This is probably the first time I don't look so much like a tourist." It was also more masculine than anything else I'd worn. My hair was back in a ponytail, and I didn't have any makeup on. I hadn't been this tan in years. I felt great and lighthearted. "Do you like it?"

She nodded appreciatively. "Very much."

I smirked. "Let's go. I'm anxious to find out more about these galleries and the plans you have for them."

For a moment, I thought she was going to hold my hand again, but once we were in public, she made sure there was enough space between us. That was odd considering we had several get-togethers around town where people could tell we were in some kind of relationship. We grabbed salads at a small deli around the corner and were sitting at her dining table twenty minutes later.

"Tell me about your new artist," I said. I wasn't jealous at all. I wanted to hear about her successes just like I wanted to share mine with her.

"His name is Bishop Meeker. He focuses a lot on sculpture which is something I'm trying to promote more. He's a graduate of the New York Academy of Art and has been working with Erich Amal."

My mouth dropped. Amal was known for his sculptures worldwide. There was even a documentary about him on one of the streaming services. "Holy shit. That's incredible. We studied Amal at school. Do you know him?"

"We've met a few times, but he really blew up in the last few years."

"This is so cool. And I'll have to google Meeker later and see what he's all about." I never got the hang of sculpting. I knew Amal was all about geometric forms. While impressive, I didn't see the world in abstract. My sculptures were mediocre work at best. I was better with a paintbrush or a pastel pencil.

"Are you excited about the fair? In a few short hours, the world is going to see some of your work," Olivia said. I liked watching her mouth when she talked. Especially when she was relaxed. Her lips were smooth and full, and I kept thinking about how well we kissed and the journey that mouth had taken over my body. Several times. "What are you thinking about?" Busted. There was no sense in telling a lie.

"Your mouth," I said. She looked a little shocked. "And I don't even care that you know."

"You're very direct."

"I don't have enough time to not be." I watched as she finished her glass of wine and pulled her bottom lip into her mouth to savor the last drop of wine. "Plus, I think you tease me a lot."

"I don't," she said.

"Really? So, you're just sexy all the time and send me fuck me signals whenever our eyes meet?"

She laughed. "I don't think I'm doing that."

"Well, then maybe it's just what I want to see." I paused for a moment. "Can we please revisit the conversation about us? You and me and what happens when I leave?" I don't know what I was expecting, but it wasn't her pushing from her chair and walking away from me. I followed her into the living room that overlooked the ocean.

"I don't want to talk about this, Josie." Her voice was raspy and her words didn't sound like her. Panic squeezed my throat, and I took a deep breath to swallow it. "We're just not in the same place. You're so young and you have your whole life in front of you."

"Please. It's worth it to at least entertain the idea."

"I'm not emotionally available for anything more than what's going on at this moment," she said.

I stood in front of her and put my hands on her crossed arms. "I don't understand why not." She pulled away and walked over to the window to stare out into the night. I could see her reflection in the glass and the emotions that played out on her face. I saw anger, regret, sadness, but when she turned around, her face was stoic.

"We've talked about this. Why can't you just let it be?"

I lifted my eyebrow. "Make me understand. Tell me why it's okay after having what I consider a great summer." I moved closer. "We're great together. Nobody's going to mesh with you as well as I do. We have so much in common but not enough to get bored quickly." I pulled her into my arms. "Providence isn't far from here or from Boston. Why can't we at least try?" She broke loose again. I felt the gravity of a breakup drift over me like a weighted blanket.

"You're so young, Josie. You have so much to experience still in this life. You're fresh out of college. What life experiences do you have?"

"Who cares? Why can't we experience them together?"

She touched my cheek. "We're just at two different places. You'll want to settle down with somebody your age and start a family and I'm past that. I've done that."

Spikes of anger poked my chest. "You're only thirty-five. And I never said I was hung up on kids. Not everyone wants them."

"Do you want a family?" She straightened her shoulders and glared at me, challenging me to say something to the contrary.

"If I fall in love with somebody and it's meant to be, then great. It's not like my main goal in life. Not everyone needs to have a kid." Did I want a family? Maybe someday. Was it a necessity? No. I wanted to fall in love more than anything, and if the person I was with wanted kids, then we would. It wasn't a make-or-break thing, and I wished Olivia would understand that.

"I'm not the person you want to have a relationship with or fall in love with." She stood in front of me with her hands on her hips. She was always challenging me.

"What if it's too late?" I asked. Doubt, uncertainty, then realization set in when she realized what I said. Oh, shit. I just told her I was in love with her in a roundabout way. Maybe she didn't catch that and was focusing on the relationship aspect, but deep down I knew she heard me. I knew she felt it in her heart that my feelings were true.

She opened her mouth, then closed it. Then she angrily left the room. I should've been hurt and dejected, but I knew the opposite was happening. If she didn't have any feelings for me, she would've blown me off. This was storming off and it was a big difference. I went back to the kitchen and finished my salad. When I was done, I rinsed my plate and hers and left her a note on the table.

Olivia,

I'm not giving up. I still have a week to show you that we belong together. Maybe it's forever, or maybe it's something we both need in our lives right now. With this little time left, I want each day to count. I hope you call me in the morning to help set up for the fair.

J

CHAPTER EIGHTEEN

I refused to go to the fair before noon. I was too nervous to check on my art and Olivia hadn't called to ask for help setting up. I hated that we went all night and all morning without texting. The silence killed me. I made my way to town by walking on the beach. There was no way I'd find parking so, unless I wanted to borrow Noah's lime green and bright blue Mongoose bicycle, I was stuck hoofing it. Instead of walking straight to the gallery, I squeezed into the coffee shop, grabbed a cup of coffee, and sat on the only available stool that faced Ocean Front.

Beth wasn't kidding when she said it would be packed. I wasn't an introvert and this many people freaked me out. I couldn't keep my eyes off Olivia. Both she and Beth had a lot of traffic. Olivia was giving potential buyers space but was close enough to answer questions. Inside the gallery she seemed so refined, but out in the streets she seemed more relaxed and approachable. I didn't hear from her last night after I left, but that didn't scare me. I meant every word I said. I wanted to spend as much time with her as possible even if at the end of it, she wanted to end things. I told myself I would be okay with her decision, but I knew it would break something fundamental inside of me. Whatever happened was going to change me forever.

My phone vibrated with a text. *Where are you?*

My heart sank when I saw the message was from Beth and not Olivia.

I'm being a total chicken and downing as much caffeine as I can across the street. I was on my third cup and was starting to get the jitters. I watched her look at her phone and squint her eyes to try to find me behind the glass. I waved. She waved for me to come over.

Come out here. I have news.

I took a deep breath and helped myself to complimentary iced water with lemon before leaving the coffee shop. "How's it going?" I couldn't look at my paintings. I was too nervous.

"Both of yours already sold." Her blue eyes sparkled with excitement, and she pulled me into a tight, happy hug.

My energy ramped up at her news. I casually glanced at Olivia who was frowning. I released Beth. "That's amazing! Really?" I wanted to play it cool, but this was too exciting for me.

She showed me the sold stickers on both tags. "Like within minutes. To a local. He just pointed to them and said sold." She clapped her hands together and laughed. "Why were you hiding in there this whole time? I could've introduced you." She didn't know this was my first art show that wasn't school related.

"It's so nerve-wracking. People judging your work. I didn't want to hear any criticism. And to see them look and then walk away without buying would have crushed me." I placed my hand on my heart to emphasize my words.

"I know. It's such a vulnerable profession, but you're killing it. You should go talk to Olivia and see how the rest of your paintings are doing." Beth excused herself to help a few customers who had wandered into the tent. I met Olivia's stare. It would've been rude and out of character for me to turn around and walk away so I threaded my way through the throngs of people until I found myself in front of her.

"How's it going?" I asked.

Her hands were on her hips as though she was mad at me and maybe she was, but I saw her brush aside those emotions. "They sold," she said. Her mouth blossomed into a genuine smile. "I told you that would happen."

My smile mirrored hers. "Really? Thank you." I hated that we went all night and all morning without texting. The silence killed me.

"You're welcome. It was a busy morning," she said.

I looked around to see how the rest of the art on display was fairing. Today was about me and art. Me and her would have to wait until after sunset. "It looks like a lot of things have already sold."

"I predict that everything will be sold by the end of the day. The buyers are supposed to swing by at six to pick all of it up, but if they don't then I'll just store it in the gallery. They can call me and pick it up whenever is convenient for them."

"Are most of the buyers locals? Or out-of-towners?"

"Mostly locals bought yours." Her unemotional stare was killing me.

"Do you want me to come back at five thirty and help you break down or help distribute the art?" My phone chimed with a text message, but I ignored it.

"We have art movers to do that, but I could use some help getting the easels and tables back in storage," she said. My phone chimed again. "You might want to answer your texts. Sounds like somebody really needs you."

I flipped my phone over and saw it was Noah. I waved the phone at Olivia. "It's Noah." Her shoulders relaxed a fraction.

You haven't come by the booth yet.

Have you sold anything?

Shit. I forgot to hit his booth first thing like I promised. *Yes. What about you? What booth are you in?*

103. Near the library.

I'm on my way. "I have to go. I promised Noah I'd buy a print."

Olivia's attention was pulled away from me when a potential buyer asked questions about a particular piece of pottery. I waved good-bye to her. She furrowed her brow at me but returned a half wave.

I found Noah standing by his photographs. He was so cute twisting his fingers and trying not to bounce from foot to foot. "Oh, my gosh. Are these yours?" I wasn't just humoring him. The kid had talent.

"I just sold another. I can't even tell you how many prints I've sold."

"Which one did you save for me?"

He held his finger up and disappeared behind one of the panels. "I think you'll like this one because we talked about cars the last time we gamed." It was a sepia toned reflection of Goda's Diner in the bumper of a rusty Studebaker.

I looked at it hard and then held it gently against my chest. "I love it, Noah. I'm so happy you're selling your art. That's such a big accomplishment."

"Look at this. Our baby boy signing his prints." Cassie, who came out of nowhere, thrust her phone at me to show me a photo of Noah. She was unbelievably proud and rightfully so. "I can't believe how good he is." The shot was of Noah chewing his bottom lip and carefully signing his name. I was proud of him, too.

"He's incredible. I knew he was excited about the class, but I think he's found his calling," I said. Brook was standing a few feet down from us with Ava asleep in her stroller. She pushed the stroller back and forth as though rocking Ava. She, too, was beaming with pride.

"He wants to try film photography, so this fall we'll get him enrolled in a class. I don't think the academy offers darkroom. Only digital," Cassie said.

"Either one would be such a valuable learning experience. Especially since he has an eye for art," I said. I looked at the sand dollar photo he took and decided I needed to have that print, too, because it reminded me of the wonderful summer I had here in Goda. I plucked it off the twine and paid for it. Noah practically pranced around me with excitement.

Cassie bumped my elbow. "That's so sweet of you," she said.

"It'll be a great reminder of this summer. I'll cherish it." I would cherish a lot about this summer. My good fortune, my time with Olivia, and the quaint town of Goda, Massachusetts, that changed my life.

By the end of the day, I was exhausted mentally and physically. I had walked Beach Street about twenty times. I bought a comfy sweatshirt that had a lobster holding a banner that said Goda. It was oversized, warm, cheesy, and I loved everything about it. It was also on sale. My life choices would be a series of what's on sale until I had the art fair money in the bank. I found myself in front of Monteclair Gallery right at five thirty. Buyers were lined up to take their art.

"What would you like me to do?" I jumped in to help.

"Once the art is out of the booth, I need help putting the shelves in the storage shed out back. The easels will go inside," Olivia said. She returned to her task of taking receipts and I stepped out of the way. Once the crowd thinned and the final piece was wrapped and handed to the new owner, I was able to fold and stack the easels. We had the area cleaned and buttoned up in no time.

"I bet you're tired," I said.

"Exhausted, but it's so worth it."

"Do you need anything?" I just wanted to make sure she was taking care of herself.

"No. Thank you for your help today."

I hated this little game of back and forth to see who would cave. I decided it wouldn't be me. I'd put it all out there for her to take if she wanted it.

❖

The air had cooled since the sun set. I put on my new sweatshirt and grabbed a flashlight. I thought about bringing some wine but decided against it. I didn't want to be too presumptuous. She was exactly where I thought she'd be—tucked up against the dune and staring off into the distance. "Feel like taking a walk?" I asked.

"Sure." She stood and brushed the sand off her pants.

I shoved my hands in my hoodie pouch and headed for the water. I stopped when I felt her hands on my elbow. "What's wrong?" I asked.

She shook her head and leaned up against me. I put my arm around her shoulder until she turned to me, and I held her in my arms. It surprised me when her body shook and I heard soft sobs against my shoulder. "I'm sorry. I'm just overly emotional today. The end of the season always makes me sad. Most people leave and while I enjoy the sparseness of activity, it also means I'll be heading back to Boston soon." She struggled to keep a sob from slipping out. "I don't like leaving this place."

"Your heart is here. I completely understand. I wish you could do all your business here, too. It's a wonderful place. I'll always remember this summer and the beauty of Monteclair beach."

She sniffled and gave a soft laugh. "It's not called Monteclair Beach."

"Well, that's what I'm calling it. This beach is special because of you," I said.

She leaned up and kissed me. It wasn't just a soft brush of her lips against mine. She clutched me and pulled my body flush against hers. It was the first time we kissed passionately in public. Granted, it was a deserted beach and at night, but she wasn't hiding anything from anybody. I gave her everything she gave me. She slipped her hands under my sweatshirt pushed my tank top up to feel my skin. I shuddered at her touch.

"Let's go back to my place," she said.

I held her elbows to steady her and to make her focus on my face and not my body. "Are you sure?"

"Yes."

The air between us felt heavy. It was sexually charged, but there was something else. The closer we got to her house, the tighter my chest felt. I didn't know if my heart was growing or if the intensity of this moment made my ribs constrict. Breathing seemed hard. I gulped in the night air and tried to blow out my breath as quietly as I could.

"Are you okay?" Olivia asked.

I realized I was a step ahead of her and slowed down. "I'm fine." I gave her a shaky smile and slipped my hand in hers. I was more than fine. I was elated and scared of feeling so vulnerable. I was giving myself to somebody who I wasn't sure wanted more than tonight. Nothing made sense right now except her. Except us.

I dropped my shoes by the door of the mudroom and followed her into the house. She kept walking until she reached her bedroom. She slipped out of her pants and unbuttoned her shirt. Her eyes were on mine the whole time. I shrugged off my sweatshirt and sat on the bed. She walked over and stood between my legs. She was soft and beautiful. Maybe she couldn't say the words because she was scared of the truth, but I was going to cherish this moment forever.

"I can't even tell you how beautiful you are." I brushed my fingertips along the skin above her panties and smiled when a trail of chill bumps popped up along her stomach and thighs.

She didn't say anything but cupped my face and bent to kiss me. I wrapped my arms around her and pulled her back onto the bed with me. I didn't need words. I could sense her emotions with every touch. This was the way she showed me she cared. It was safe and private. Tonight, was different. It felt like the first and last time with her and I willed myself not to cry. She slipped off her hair tie and I smiled briefly as her hair fell around us. I threaded my fingers through it and gently pulled her mouth to mine. Because I knew our time was almost up, I stretched out every minute, every second and relished every part of her body. I kissed her lips, her cheeks, the small mole by her ear, and the sensitive spot on her neck that had her grabbing at my tank. I rolled her over and nestled my hips between her legs.

"Do you want this off?" I looked down at my tank top stretched and gathered in her hands.

"Oh, yes," Olivia said. I wanted to smile and be flirty like I normally was, but the vibe was different. I leaned up on my knees, lifted the shirt off, and threw it somewhere behind us. Her hands were quick to touch my bare skin. "You're so warm. You're always so warm."

"I love…this lace," I said. My brain hiccupped halfway through my sentence. I didn't want her to shut down and end the evening before I had a chance to show her how I felt. She didn't want my words, but she wanted my touch.

Even though we hadn't spoken most of the day, I knew I would end up here tonight, and she did as well. She was wearing my favorite bra and panty set. It was the most delicate lace I'd ever touched, and it felt as soft as her skin. I ran my hands over her thighs and watched as she spread them wider. Every time my fingers got close to the juncture, her breath hitched. Her hips tilted up and she licked her lips, but she wasn't going to ask. I slipped my thumbs under the small gap where her panties touched her thigh and brushed them against her swollen pussy. Her first moan made my insides soft. Her second moan was gritty and powerful as I slipped inside her. She was slick, tight, and warm. I wanted her panties off, but watching her hips move against my hand while the lace was pulled aside reminded me of how sexual Olivia was and how she wasn't ashamed of pleasure. She slipped her hand inside her panties and massaged her clit while I slipped both thumbs inside her. She was tight, wet, and after a few moments, I needed more. I had to see her touch herself.

I carefully pulled her panties off and spread her apart like she was before. She didn't disappoint me. Watching her rub her finger up and down her slit and moving it fast over her clit made me weak. I slipped two fingers inside, careful not to disturb her movement but add to her pleasure. She spread her legs wider and when her hand moved faster, I stopped her. I wasn't ready for her to come yet. I thought she'd be upset, but she put her hands up above her head and pressed her palms against the headboard.

I slid down the bed and swirled my tongue around her swollen clit while still moving inside her. Her legs started shaking and she pressed her hips against my mouth. I held them down with one hand and kept moving until she came hard. I felt the fast pulse as her pussy clenched and unclenched during her orgasm. I didn't want her overly sensitive because it was so early in the night and hoped to make love to her several more times. I stopped and moved up beside her.

She turned and pressed her face against my shoulder. We were both breathing so hard that I didn't know if the noises she was making were soft sobs or deep breaths. Were there tears on my shoulder or was she sweating?

"Are you okay?" I felt her nod against my neck and pulled the covers up around us. It was unlike her to snuggle against me so I held her in my arms and waited. When I heard her quietly sniffle, I knew those were tears. I didn't want to react for fear of ruining the moment.

Olivia was delicate and even though we'd had lots of sex, this was the first time that I knew her heart was in it, too. I kissed her forehead and tightened my grip on her. I didn't want tonight to end. I wanted her to profess her love, but my heart sank when I knew that wasn't going to happen. I was going to have to enjoy tonight as though it was our last because it probably was.

"The best part about being with you is that your body responds to my touch as though we're in sync," I said. It wasn't a profession of undying love, but I wanted her to know that I felt it, too. Maybe I never took the time to get to know my lover's body before because I was always in such a rush to get off, or maybe it was because I was truly in love for the first time in my life. I paid attention to her body and learned how to move with her to give her the most pleasure.

"It's nice," she said.

I rolled my eyes. I knew she couldn't see me with her head below mine. Nice was a stupid word especially after sex. It was a dismissive word. Yes, you look nice today or yes, the weather is nice. I wasn't going to challenge her though. I was going to take every morsel she offered.

She moved on her side so her head was on my shoulder and one of her legs was between mine. She fit me perfectly. We were quiet for about five minutes, and I thought she'd fallen asleep until I felt her fingers flutter over my breast and down my side.

"Mmm. That feels good," I said. It felt even better when she dipped her hand inside my soaking wet boxers and rubbed her fingers up and down my wet slit.

"I can't believe you're still dressed," she said. With her emotions in check, she looked at me for the first time since her orgasm.

I tried to smile and slip into my happy-go-lucky self, but my heart was fully exposed and there for her to take and she ignored it. I shrugged instead. "Tonight isn't about me."

She kissed the corner of my mouth. "I think it is."

My mouth turned down at the corners, but I caught it before a full frown set into place. We both had the same goal of pleasing one another without saying any words. I wanted to scream that it was about us and this relationship deserved a chance, but I kept quiet and closed my eyes.

I lifted my hips so she could pull down my boxers. When she slipped two fingers inside, I pressed against her hands. Her eyes darkened with desire as I watched her through slitted eyelids. She enjoyed my body and the control she had over it. I tightened my grip around her shoulders to keep her near me. I wanted to hold her when I came, but she moved out of my embrace. When her tongue hit my clit, I gritted my teeth and held onto the orgasm for as long as I could. Her mouth was warm, wet, and felt incredible on my skin. She felt wonderful and I rolled into my orgasm as smooth as the silk sheets I clutched in my hands.

"Damn, I'm going to miss you," I said.

Olivia turned me on my stomach and licked her way up my body from the tender spot behind my knees to the tenderness of my neck. She scraped her teeth on the sensitive area below my ear and sucked my shoulder hard. It was hard to process what I was feeling physically and emotionally.

"You are an amazing young woman," she said.

She was focusing on the age thing again and even though it bothered me, I wasn't going to let it get between us. Not tonight. I knew my time with Olivia was limited. I felt her fingers graze my slit and I lifted my hips and spread my legs to give her better access. She knelt in the space between my legs and pressed her chest into my back. She bit my neck softly when she entered me. I hissed at the intense pleasure and bucked against her hand until another orgasm rippled through my body. I was simultaneously exhausted and never felt so alive and so alone before. Tonight was fucking with my head and my heart.

I pulled her into my arms so that we were spooning. She grabbed the blankets and covered us. Every time she touched me, I wanted to plead my case about continuing our relationship, but we both drifted off to sleep. She was gone when I woke up but left me a note on the counter next to the coffee maker.

Josie,

Thank you for a beautiful night. I can't tell you what this friendship has done for me. You made me believe in living again and I can't thank you enough. I look forward to hearing about your success as an artist in the upcoming years.

Sincerely,

Olivia

I scoffed when I read the word friendship again. This note could've been left for anyone, not somebody she just had multiple orgasms with hours before. And sincerely? That word could fuck right off. I went from gloriously happy to pissed off in three seconds. I left the letter exactly where I found it and stormed out.

CHAPTER NINETEEN

"The fall festival is the biggest thing that Meyers participates in all year long." Emily stared at me as though I was bananas for not wanting to volunteer to run the booth for the Providence Pumpkin Patch Festival that ran the third weekend in October. The businesses in Corporate Woods set up booths in the park across the street that offered fun activities for families who worked in the complex. The volunteers at Meyers filled out a schedule of when they wanted to sell pumpkins and apple cider doughnuts, or paint faces, or pop kettle corn.

I was perfectly content hiding in my studio apartment every weekend until summer, eating mac and cheese and sketching the neighbor's cat, Tilly. Every night Tilly stared at me from outside my kitchen window until I let her in. I was on the third floor, and seeing her perched outside my window on the fire escape gave me heart palpitations. I had made bad decision after bad decision since leaving Goda. I regretted accepting this job. I regretted living in a building that had paper-thin walls and a questionable furnace. I felt the downward spiral the moment Goda was in my rearview mirror.

"I have a lot going on right now." I didn't but I also didn't have the heart to do extracurricular activities for a job I didn't like.

"It'll look really good to the higher-ups if you volunteer. Plus, if you sign up, we can work together this weekend to face-paint. It'll be good experience," Emily said.

Sure, face-painting would look amazing on my résumé. I blinked hard to keep my eyes from rolling. "Fine. Sign me up for Saturday. Do I need to bring paints?"

Emily waved me off. "Oh, I have plenty. This is so exciting! You might want to practice. I'll send you a link to some of the face paintings I've done over the last couple of years."

Never mind that I was up against a deadline. A customer wanted options on his new Hawaiian-themed restaurant. Everyone was trying to come up with a clever logo while I was working on a mural design for the eating area. It was affordable island cuisine and focused on family time. It was our most exciting job to date. Our meeting with the customer was Friday. I was very pleased with my design, but I had yet to show it to my team. I was basically a paid intern with very little say in decisions. Emily had been with the company for three years and we were almost at the same level. It didn't look good for my future.

"I can look online, too. I'm sure the kids want dragons, princesses, jack-o-lanterns, witches, and everything Halloween, right?" I asked.

"Yeah, I guess it's pretty obvious, huh?"

I shrugged. "Kids are pretty predictable." Maybe being around Noah and his friends a few times over the summer helped me figure out what kids liked. I tuned Emily out and stared at Noah's photograph. It was the only personal item I had in my cubicle. I looked at it often and wondered how Olivia was doing. That last night we shared was the last time I spoke with her. Brook and Cassie were wrong. Olivia didn't want me. The summer was good enough for her even though my heart ached in an unfamiliar way.

"We can do morning or afternoon."

"Afternoon. I'm not a morning person," I said. It was a good thing we had flex time here at Meyers. Seven thirty was just too early for me to function.

"Okay, great. We're on from one to four. Just maybe show up a few minutes early and I can show you around," Emily said. She was nice. I liked her, but she was a bit much. She liked to talk and I liked to brood. I appreciated her attempts to engage me in conversation though. We were the only women in the creative department.

I forced a smile. "Great. I'll meet you here at twelve forty-five." She gave me a fist bump and turned back around to finish her project on car wax. I worked on the mural until I had something that was presentable. I emailed it to my boss and turned off the lights before I locked up. I was almost always the last one out. Not because I was an overachiever; I just had nowhere else to be.

Tilly was waiting for me when I unlocked the door. Her shadow fell across the hardwood floor ominously. I scolded her and raced to the window. "Get in here. How long have you been waiting?" Her orange fur felt cool to the touch. I buried my face in her neck. "You're the best thing that's happened to me here." I gave her a quick kiss and put her on the counter. "We're running out of treats you like, but I picked up freeze-dried minnows. Apparently, all the kitties are raving about them." I ripped the perforated top and leaned back as the pungent smell wafted up and filled my nostrils. I blew out a breath and coughed. "Here you go." I gave her one that she sniffed and after five long seconds of contemplating whether or not she was interested, gingerly took it, and hopped off the counter.

My phone dinged with new email notification. I grabbed a beer and plopped down on my new-to-me couch my old roommate was going to put out on the curb. The message in my inbox made me sit up straighter. It was another commissioned work. Brook's sister-in-law Erica finally wanted portraits of her children. I could use the extra cash with the holidays coming up.

Erica,

It's so nice to hear from you. I'm very interested, and I can meet you this weekend either in person or via Zoom. Please call or text me. I'm scheduled to work at my office's fall festival Saturday afternoon, but that is my only obligation.

Sincerely,

Josie

That sounded professional enough. I wondered how the Wellingtons were doing. Noah and I gamed from time to time. Cassie texted me anytime they had people over to tell me how their guests gushed over the portraits. She also said she wanted to have lunch soon. Wellington Enterprises was opening up a new grocery store only a few miles from my studio this spring. Cassie was somehow involved. I knew she worked on environmental stuff, but I didn't know why she was involved in a grocery store. I didn't care. It would be good to see her again. My friends from RISD seemed so distant. We weren't the same people we were when we graduated. The summer changed me and I didn't know if I liked the new me or not.

"Wow. That's an amazing dragon!" Emily peered over my shoulder and watched as I transformed Rosaline's son's sweet, innocent face into to a fire-breathing dragon with fierce eyes and red and yellow flames streaming from his mouth. It was probably too much and took a lot of time, but you couldn't rush art. Some of the kids in my line got restless and moved over to Emily's. She was doing a great job making pixies, butterflies, and ladybugs.

It took me twenty minutes to finish and when I was done, Emily took several photos. I was proud of it and the kid was beyond excited.

"I can't wait to show my mom," he said and dashed off.

"Good job, Josie," Emily said. Her voice didn't hold any jealousy. The next boy in line wanted the same thing so I spent the rest of my afternoon painting blue, gold, and red dragons.

Four o'clock finally came and I was cleaning my brushes when I heard a familiar voice. "Josie!"

I looked up. "Noah! What on earth are you doing here?" I gave him a hug. I swore he got taller in two months.

"Mom's company has a booth on the other side of the park." He pointed in the opposite direction. I didn't realize they had an office in Corporate Woods.

"That's wonderful. How are you? How's school?" I hated that people always asked kids that. I hurried with a follow-up question. "Have you played any new games? I got the new *Super Mario Brothers*," I said.

"I got it last week, but I've been too busy to play it," he said.

"It's pretty good. When you get some time, text me and we'll play." I felt like a slug. I worked and gamed and that was my life. "Oh, I might paint your cousins for your aunt." I hadn't done anything with my art since I moved back to Providence. I was too depressed.

"Yeah, she loves the ones you did of me and Ava. Mom brought them back to Boston. They're in the house. Now everyone can see them. Including my friends." He muttered that last part under his breath.

"I'm sorry if it embarrasses you for your friends to see."

The tips of his ears turned pink. "No. It's fine." He sniffled and rubbed his nose as though he suffered from allergies. He bounced from foot to foot as though he had places to go but was staying in the conversation to be polite.

"Go have a good time. It was so good to see you again. Tell Brook and Cassie I said hello," I said.

He pulled out his phone. "I just sent them a pin so they'll know how to find you. Are you done here?"

I nodded. "Unless you want me to paint your face into a dragon." Emily swooped in and showed him a photo of the first one I did. He hesitated. I could see him struggle with getting excited about having a dragon face and being too old for one. "Hey, it's okay. We've put up most of our brushes. Maybe next time." I didn't want to pressure him. I waved when Brook and Cassie strolled up with Ava. "I'm so excited to see you all."

"How are you?" Brook asked. She looked at the banner in front of the table. "How's the new job?" Emily was far enough away and too busy cleaning up to pay us any attention, but I still wasn't in a position to answer honestly. I shrugged. She got the hint. "Are you excited to be back in Providence?" She was asking all the wrong questions. My life sucked since I left Goda.

"It's nice to be able to afford basic things like food, but I miss beach life. Oh, I heard from Erica."

"That's great. She was worried about bothering you since you got a new job," Cassie said.

"I haven't really done anything artsy since this summer so I'm excited to work with her. Her daughters are adorable," I said.

"They're so cute. Makes me want to have another," Cassie said. She kissed Brook's cheek before Brook had a chance to weigh in. "I'm just teasing. Ava and Noah are enough."

Ava heard her name and shouted, "Bounce!"

Brook smiled. "It was good to see you, Josie. We need to hurry up and get over to the bouncy houses before they deflate them, but I do want to talk to you about something. Are you available tomorrow afternoon?"

"Definitely. Any particular time?"

"How about grabbing drinks down at Metropolis? Around five?"

"Sounds perfect." It was going to be hard to wait because I was super intrigued by what Brook wanted from me.

"See you later," Cassie said. Ava even waved to me as they strolled off.

"Aren't those the Wellingtons?" Emily asked. She watched as they disappeared into the thinning crowd. "Didn't you do a residency with them?" She turned to me. "That whole family is too pretty."

"I know, right?" Five o'clock tomorrow couldn't come soon enough. Did they want me to paint something for them? Another portrait? A family portrait? "Do you need me to do anything here or are we done?"

Emily smiled. "Nope. We're done. You did great today. The kids loved your dragons."

"Your fairies were great, too," I said. She was good, but it was obvious her skill was computer-generated and not freestyle like mine. I grabbed my messenger bag. "Thanks for inviting me. This was fun." I didn't want to do it again, but it was nice to get out in the fresh, crisp air instead of holing up in my studio. I drove home anxious for tomorrow evening.

"Are you happy with your job?" Brook and I were tucked in a corner booth at Metropolis drinking dry martinis. I was on edge waiting for her to start the dialogue. That wasn't the question I was expecting.

"I mean, it's a decent job with good benefits. Am I happy?" Oh, fuck. What if she knew Meyers? She didn't strike me as somebody who would snitch.

"What was your goal after your residency with us?" she asked.

"Ideally, I wanted to find a job where I could study under another artist and learn more from them. But those kinds of internships are extremely hard to land. You have to know the right people and get in on the ground floor. Plus, they tend to be unpaid or underpaid. I don't have the luxury of taking those positions."

"So your current job isn't what you envisioned?" she asked.

"Don't get me wrong, my job as junior creative designer at Meyers is great." I was starting to panic.

Brook held up her hand. "Okay, I'm going to cut to the chase. I'd like to offer you a position with Wellington Enterprises within our creative department as a creative liaison. That includes working with Cassie at our Green Alliance Organization. I don't want to pull you away from something if you're happy, but it sounds like you would be open to something different."

I sat back in the booth stunned by her words. Of all the things I was expecting, this wasn't on the list. "Wow. I'm shocked. Why?" I shook my head. "I mean, that's amazing."

Brook's laugh reminded me of Olivia's. "One of our artists left to raise her family and a spot opened up. We thought of you immediately." Once again, the Wellingtons were proving to be too good to be true.

"Tell me about it. What's the office environment like? Is there a benefits package?" I didn't want to look desperate, but I couldn't think of any other questions to ask.

"It's a creative department so things are pretty open and casual. And it's not a nine-to-five job. As long as you put in your hours, we're happy. If you're interested, I can have human resources send you a packet of information this week."

"I'm definitely interested. Where's the position? Providence, or in Boston or Hartford?" I couldn't remember all the cities in the northeast where they had an office.

"The creative department is in Boston. You could commute or move to Boston. You live north of Providence, right? That'll cut down on commute time." She waved her hand at me. "Cassie has the details figured out since you already live here. Or use your signing bonus to get out of your lease and move to Boston," she said.

Signing bonus? Shut up. I was twenty-three years old. Who was I to get a signing bonus? My anxiety was quickly replaced by panic. I couldn't even afford a studio in downtown Providence. How was I going to be able to afford Boston? Even if I stayed here, I'd need a new car because my Toyota wasn't going to make it much longer. I could ignore the oil spots on the street for only so long.

Brook touched my hand bringing me back to the present. "Don't worry about anything. We have studios in town that we rent out to our employees. Our benefits are great, and the salary will be competitive." She softened. "I know how hard it is to get started fresh out of college and we take pride in taking care of our employees." She held up a finger and quickly typed something on her phone. I took several sips of my drink and thought about everything I'd have to do to make this happen. "You'll have your contract in the morning."

I slowly shook my head in disbelief. "You and Cassie are just too good to me."

"You're talented and you're smart. Wellington is getting the better end of this deal." She waved a hand. "Besides, my whole family loves you. Noah talks about you all the time. We're so thankful that you're still such a positive force in his life. He'll come down to dinner and tell us Josie did this or Josie did that during one of your games."

"He's such a great kid. I love how much he loves school and how he's still into photography."

"We have the best children. Ava's getting ready to turn three and she's pretty chill for a toddler. But then Cassie's pretty relaxed, too. I'm so happy Ava has her gentle disposition," Brook said.

"And Noah has yours," I said. I knew Brook had a soft side even though everyone in my world who claimed to know her called her an ice queen. A flash of memory of Olivia streaked across my mind. The first time we made love I playfully called her an ice queen. My emotions must have flickered across my face because Brook's voice changed.

"How are you holding up?" Brook asked. I wasn't going to pretend that I didn't know what she meant. She deserved more respect than that.

"It's been hard. My heart's in a weird place. I haven't felt inspired since I left Goda. I'm glad Erica reached out because that might be the boost I need," I said. I hadn't even unpacked any of my art supplies since moving to my studio.

"If it's any consolation, Olivia's been extremely down since you left. We've seen her twice now and both times she didn't seem like herself."

I raised my eyebrows at the news, but I knew nothing I could say or do would change Olivia's mind. I was out of her life and there wasn't anything I could do about it. "I tried everything. I begged, I told her how great we were together, I showed her how great we were, and she still shut me down."

Brook squeezed my hand. "She's wrong. We all know it, but she has to come to that conclusion on her own. Maybe she has.

Maybe she's punishing herself for having a relationship after the accident. You can't let her dictate your own happiness though."

"I know. When I accepted your residency I told myself not to have a relationship with anyone because I needed to focus on my art. I'm an idiot for falling in love with her."

Brook's eyebrow raised at my confession. "Love, huh?" She leaned back in her chair. "Well, that changes everything."

CHAPTER TWENTY

Even though I wasn't feeling it, I got dolled up for the Wellington Enterprises corporate holiday party held at the Skyline Hotel in Boston. I owed it to Cassie and Brook. They went through hoops to get me settled into my life here. I could've commuted, especially because Cassie had me scheduled to design murals in the organic grocery stores that were popping up in Rhode Island, Connecticut, and Massachusetts in the spring. But it just made sense to be closer to the office.

"This is such a beautiful hotel. I've been waiting for this all year," Ashton said. She worked in the Boston office in the marketing department. We hit it off my first week. She was smart, perky, and completely in love with her boyfriend. That was annoying to hear continuously, but I couldn't blame her. She found somebody who loved her just as much as she loved them.

"Oh? Are they famous for great parties?" I already knew the answer because their summer party was amazing and that was just a private barbecue.

She put her hand on her hip and rolled her eyes. "Stop it. You know they are. Look at this. How much money did they drop on this?" She pointed to an oversized plush red velvet chair with ornate golden arms and legs. "I bet you they hired the real Santa."

I nudged her with my elbow. "Shut up." I laughed but sobered up when the dude they hired looked exactly like he walked out of a Norman Rockwell painting. "Huh. You're probably not wrong."

She elbowed me back. "See? Come on. Let's grab some food and find a place to sit." She waved at a few employees already seated from her department. This was one of the reasons I didn't want to come. I worked with them. Even though I liked them and knew most of them, I didn't want to sit with them, too. It felt too much like being at work.

"Josie, over here!" I turned to see who was calling my name. Noah, wearing slacks, a button-down shirt with a cashmere sweater over it, and chukka boots, waved me over.

"Oh, my goodness. Look at you. You're like all grown up." He had grown at least an inch since I saw him at the pumpkin patch festival. It was so hard not to squeeze him or pull him into a hug, especially since he was surrounded by kids his age. I leaned closer. "Sorry. I didn't mean to embarrass you."

His smile was alarmingly charming. "You didn't. It's good to see you." He nodded his head toward Ashton who had sat down with our co-workers. "Is that your new girlfriend?"

"Oh, no. She's a co-worker. We're just friends." I looked around. "What about you? Is your date here?" The kid blushed immediately and scuffed his shoe on the marble floor as though he was embarrassed. It was so adorable and innocent.

"I'm not dating," he said.

"I heard you're killing it in film photography." His blue eyes lit up and his joy was so big that I got lost in his excitement.

"It's the best. Mom and Cassie converted one of the upstairs bathrooms into a dark room. I'm learning how to develop film."

"That's amazing," I said.

"Next year I can take a filmmaking class. I'm so excited to make movies," he said.

"You're making movies now, my dude. I've seen your videos on Instagram." I knew his moms were a hard no on TikTok.

"Thanks." He nodded. "The class I took in Goda was so much fun. I learned a lot, too."

"You're so talented. I have your photograph up in my cubicle at work and so many people say how great it is."

"Which one? The bumper or the sand dollar?"

The sand dollar was at home. Looking at it reminded me of Olivia and the beach. Sometimes I teared up when I saw it so I couldn't bring it to the office. "The bumper. Everyone asks if a well-known photographer took it. I tell them yes."

"Aw, you're playing with me."

I shook my head. "Nope. True story. It's wonderful." I loved this kid.

We both sharply turned at the sound of glass crashing on the marble floor.

"Oh, someone dropped a glass," Noah said.

He turned back around, but I was frozen in place. Olivia was standing in line for a drink. She was wearing a form-fitting black dress that showed a hint of cleavage and her hair was styled in an updo with some curled strands pulled down. She was breathtaking. I soaked her all in. What was she doing here? I turned around in fear that she would find me staring.

Noah was going on about something. Cassie must've seen the sheer panic in my expression because she came over as soon as our eyes met.

"Josie, I'm so happy you came." She pulled me into a hug until she felt me relax a bit. "Noah, I'm going to steal Josie for a moment." I gave him a quick smile before Cassie escorted me over to their table. I was surprised to see Erica there. She stood and hugged me.

"You look fantastic," Erica said. She and Cassie had a quick exchange of looks and Erica motioned for me to sit next to her. "How's the job?" She poured a glass of champagne and handed it to me. I didn't like champagne, but out of respect and curiosity, I took a sip. It tasted clean and refreshing and smooth. This wasn't the Brut I drank in college.

"I love it," I said. "And I'm not just saying that because Brook and Cassie are here and you're family. I love that Cassie is giving me artistic freedom."

"Oh?" She was giving me extreme attention including stellar eye contact and that made me nervous. Something was happening behind me, but I wasn't going to turn around. "Tell me more about it."

"I've designed murals for three grocery stores. I'm focusing on people in that community and what's popular but also something that can stand the test of time."

"I think that's great. I love that you're getting to do more of what you really want to." She patted my hand. "And thank you so much for getting my portraits done before Christmas. I know you had a lot going on with the move and new job," she said. I'd delivered them this past weekend and Erica promptly hid them from her family. It was going to be a gift for her husband.

"Thank you for giving me a swift kick to get back into it." I spent Thanksgiving Day with my parents but the rest of the extended weekend finishing up Erica's portraits. My heart wasn't totally in it, but I liked the outcome and Erica was pleased. I loved that the Wellington family had so much faith in me and my ability. Even my parents were impressed with my career path and lucrative side business.

"You're so good. I can't wait to show them off to my friends." She paused and tilted her head to look around me. Her voice got quiet. "I don't know if you're aware of this, but Olivia is here."

I gave a small nod. My hands felt clammy and my stomach twisted inside at hearing Olivia's name. I was happy to be sitting down. If I could just make it through the next hour or two without bumping into her, I could leave without being rude. It was a big ballroom with a ton of people. The fact that I saw her at all was equally terrifying and tragic. I didn't know why she was here. She wasn't on the Wellingtons' payroll. But then, neither was Erica and yet here they both were. When Erica sat up straight and looked behind me, I stiffened. I knew Olivia was behind me. I took a deep breath and watched the reactions around the table. Cassie and Brook stood and smiled. Yep. Olivia was here. So many emotions flooded my heart, but the one that sucker-punched me was sadness.

"Olivia, we're so glad you made it," Cassie said.

I couldn't ignore her forever. I could, but it would have been immature, and I spent all last summer trying to convince her that age was just a number. I turned in my chair to be respectful, but I couldn't stand. My knees were weak. I waited until Brook and Cassie hugged her. God, she was beautiful. I'd forgotten how dark her eyes were and how soft and full her hair always looked. When she finally made eye contact, I forced a smile.

"Hello, Olivia. You're looking well." That's what people said, right? After somebody smashed your heart and refused to talk to you ever again. It was non-confrontational and completely harmless. And I wasn't lying. She was beautiful, whether she was wearing a wisp of a bra and panty set or a full-length gown. Her hair was longer, which I liked, and her nail polish a pale gold.

She put her hand on my shoulder. "It's really good to see you again," she said. She had no right to touch me.

I grew hot and bit the inside of my cheeks as her fingertips brushed softly on my skin. I dismissed her by turning back around and reaching for my champagne. She got the hint and dropped her hand.

"When did you get back into town?" Cassie asked. She linked her arm with Olivia's and walked her over to an empty seat next to her. That put her directly in my line of vision. I wanted to puke.

"Last weekend. It took me longer than usual to close up the house."

I stared at her for a solid two seconds before I broke eye contact. I turned to Erica. "I'm going to go find my friend that I came with. I'm sure she's saved me a seat and is probably looking for me."

Erica put her hand on my knee. "Don't leave. Don't let her win." Her voice was low, but she was aware of how desperately I wanted to flee. "Let's talk about something for five minutes and then you can go. Don't give her the satisfaction."

I took a deep breath and nodded. "I don't know what to talk about." Panic bubbled up in my throat.

"First of all, smile like I just said the most hilarious thing. Don't laugh because you'll sound like a hyena and then we'll all know you're struggling." That made me genuinely smile. She squeezed my hand. "Just like that. Okay. So, let me tell you a story about the time I got stuck in a freezer at my husband's restaurant." I smiled again. She laughed. "Perfect." She launched into this huge story that had me focused on her and not Olivia. Erica was a great storyteller. I didn't think anything could get my mind off Olivia, but Erica did. "And so now enough time has passed that you can get up and go see your friends without letting a certain someone know they got to you."

I hugged her because I was struggling to keep my emotions in check and she had stepped up to help me out. "Thank you." I slipped away before anyone could stop me. I weaved my way through round tables.

Ashton moved her purse from the chair she was saving for me. "Damn, I didn't know you were that tight with the Wellingtons."

I plopped down and pushed away the plate of food in front of me. "We had a good summer and I've done some work for Brook's sister-in-law." I avoided looking at their table. I wanted to go. "Look, don't hate me, but I don't feel so good so I'm going to go." I put my hand on my stomach to emphasize my point. When Ashton put her hand on my shoulder out of concern, it didn't bother me.

"Oh, no. I'm so sorry to hear that. Is there anything I can get you?"

"No, thanks." I thumbed behind us. "I'm just going to grab my coat and go. I'll see you Monday." She hugged me and I waved to the rest of the people at my table. "Have fun tonight."

With as much dignity as I could muster, I walked over to the coat room, handed the staff member my ticket, and pulled up my Lyft app to order a car. I had eight minutes. I needed fresh, cool air. I slipped into my wool coat and walked out the front door. It was cold and another round of snow began to fall. I looked up and watched as the fat snowflakes fell around me. The street would be covered in an hour. Going home now was the smart thing to do. My Lyft driver pulled up three minutes early. A hand came out of nowhere and slammed the door shut as I opened it.

Olivia was standing beside me. "Don't go." It sounded like a command which pissed me off even more. I opened the door again. She shut it. Her clipped voice had softened. "Please don't go. I want to talk to you."

"Are you getting in or no?" The Lyft driver rolled down the back window.

Olivia bent down to address him. "No. Sorry for the confusion."

He threw up his hands and drove off. I stood there staring after him because he was the last step in my plan to get as far away from Olivia as I could.

"Josie. Please turn around," she said.

I couldn't. Fuck the tears that welled up in my eyes. I wanted to be strong and as ice queeny as she was with emotions, but it was hard. I couldn't understand how somebody who painted and who loved that passionately could be so callous and indifferent about me.

I turned around. "What, Olivia, what?" I threw up my hands with indignation. "I'm pretty sure we have zero to talk about. You made that pretty clear three months ago." I tried to walk past but she stood in front of me. I took a step back. I felt trapped and began pacing.

"Can we go somewhere and talk?"

"About what?" I pronounced each syllable clearly and loudly. I was losing control. My tears betrayed me and fell onto my cheeks, but I pretended to be stoic. What I didn't expect was to see tears in her eyes, too. That stopped me from storming off. I huffed out my anger, relaxed my shoulders, and lowered my voice. "Seriously, there's nothing to talk about. You made it clear where you stood on things. On us."

Snowflakes were falling faster. A few clung to Olivia's ridiculously long eyelashes and I wanted to wipe them away, but that was the old us. The new us weren't a thing and touching her was off the table. Every time she moved closer, I stepped back.

She held up her hands. "I just need to say some things that I know I should have said sooner. You know how difficult my life has been the last three and half years. That's not an excuse, it's an explanation. Can we please go somewhere and talk?"

I didn't feel the cold. The snow was pretty but annoying and I pointed to a bench just down the block from the hotel.

She cocked her head. "Okay, we can do it here." Her coat was thin and I knew she must have been freezing but I wasn't willing to drag this out.

As soon as we sat, I turned to her. "What, Olivia? What do you need to get off your chest to make yourself feel better?" Damn. I didn't know I had it in me to be bitchy, but here I was striking out at every chance I got.

"I get that you're mad and rightfully so. The summer meant so much to me. More than you'll ever know or understand." She put her hand on mine when she saw I was starting to get worked up. "I know it meant a lot to you, too. I'm not trying to compare our experiences. Nobody will ever understand what I went through this summer or the summers before, not even you. That's just a fact."

I blew out a tense breath. "You're right. I'm sorry."

"I never thought I would ever open up to anyone again. I've had more heartache than anyone should have to deal with ever. So many people have tried to be my friend and help me through this, but I pushed them away. And then you blew into town. You were honest and bold and bright. Your light is what I needed to spark something inside of me and even though I fought it, you gave me a reason to live again." She closed her eyes and sighed. "I'm not explaining myself well. I'm terrible at words right now."

I knew she was apologizing and trying to make amends. We were in the same town and would probably run into each other from time to time. It was better to be on neutral ground and get everything we needed to say off our chests, but I still was bitter because when I tried to do this very thing, she blew me off. "Why are you so scared of me?" I asked. I couldn't look at her. I stared straight ahead.

"Because you make me feel things more powerful than I ever have before and I thought I was betraying my family. I thought that by loving you, I wasn't honoring them." She sniffled.

I stood and started pacing again. What did that mean? She loved me as in past tense? When was she feeling that way? How was she feeling now? Before I could get my questions out, somehow the word love got through the tiniest crack in the wall around my heart and shredded me. I started sobbing. I couldn't stop. I tried to walk away, but she grabbed my hand and pulled me to her.

"Don't go. Please. I'm not done."

I squeezed my eyes shut trying to stop the tears from pouring out, but my heart was stronger than my will. I barely choked out a question. "Why are you doing this to me?"

She held my face in her hands and her thumbs wiped away the tears on my cheeks. "Josie, look at me." I blinked until her face came into focus. "I'm doing this because I love you and I was stupid to let you go. I was scared that somebody as young as you could break through so easily."

I stopped crying. "What?"

"I love you. With all my heart. I know I have a lot of making up to do, but I will if you give me the chance." She started crying and that was the cue my heart needed to push out more of my own tears. "I'm so sorry I hurt you. Will you please forgive me?"

My heart felt her words and raced the information to my brain. My stomach quivered at how close her body was, and I knew in that moment that she needed me as much as I needed her. Was this really happening? I gulped in the cold air and looked at her. She was telling the truth. This was the most vulnerable she'd ever been with me. I pulled her into my arms and clutched her against me.

"This better be happening. This can't be a dream," I said. Her hair smelled like orange blossoms, and even though we were in the cold with snow coming down all around us, her body felt warm.

She leaned back to look into my eyes. "It's a dream come true."

"How are you so sappy all of a sudden?" I asked. We both laughed and sniffled.

She wrapped her arms around my waist and shrugged. "You made me this way."

I put my forehead against hers, closed my eyes, and soaked in this moment. She touched my cheek and brushed her lips against mine.

"Get out of the street before you get hit! It would be a terrible tragedy!" a woman yelled.

I looked over Olivia's shoulder to see Cassie and Brook watching us from the hotel porte cochere. I waved to them and pulled Olivia onto the sidewalk. Cassie gave me a thumbs-up.

"Yes, let's not get hit before we can start our lives together," Olivia said.

"Are you sure about this?" I put my hand over my heart as though it threatened to leave my body if she backed out now.

She locked her fingers behind my neck and kissed me hard. Her lips were cold from the air and the snow that swirled around us, but her mouth was hot and familiar. She pulled away long enough to answer. "Definitely."

I pulled her flush against me. "You know I've loved you since our first get-together, right?" I asked.

"You mean our first date?"

I playfully rolled my eyes at her. "Oh, now you want to call it a date?"

"Honestly, I knew it then, too," she said. I looked into her eyes. She was telling the truth. "I wasted a lot of time and I'm sorry."

I nuzzled her neck and kissed the soft spot on her neck that made her moan softly. "Well, how about we go somewhere and make up for lost time?" As much as I loved my studio, it wasn't really a place to take Olivia. "How far away do you live?"

"Only a few miles."

"Are you regretting sending my Lyft driver away?" Before I had a chance to order one, a limo slowly pulled up in front of us.

The driver popped out. "Hello, ladies. Mrs. Wellington asked me to take you wherever you want." He raced to our side and opened the door.

"We don't need to go very far," Olivia said. She rattled off her address and snuggled next to me in the limo.

It was the perfect ending to my heartache and the perfect beginning of us. I was never going to let her go. She was right. I was living the dream. I realized that I hadn't told her what she needed to hear the most. "I forgive you, Olivia."

EPILOGUE

It's so good to be back on Monteclair Beach," I said.
Olivia's arms circled my waist. She pressed her cheek against my back and leaned against me. It was our first weekend back in Goda after a fantastic winter together in Boston. We spent most of the day setting up the gallery and spent the night making love by the fireplace, in the shower, and in the master bed. I was exhausted, but being back here invigorated my soul. I belonged here, with Olivia. This would always be our special place.

"But it's not called Monteclair Beach," she said.

I pulled her around so that she stood in front of me. "I don't even care what the name is. This feels like home." I was treading lightly as to not upset her and the balance she had with wonderful and tragic memories. "I mean, I love your place in Boston, but being here just seems so right."

"It's too bad you're commuting."

Olivia had wanted me to quit my job and study under her, but I explained I needed this job to feel self-worth. Plus, I actually liked it. I was on my second mural in Providence. The first one was a massive hit and I felt like I was doing something with my skill. I still had the commissioned work as a solid side business, but it would be a while before I could paint full-time and feel like I was financially sound. The Ashfords recently asked me to paint a scene of their beach house that they could hang in their Providence estate. They wanted it to be large enough to hang above their settee and were willing to pay a lot of money for it. I was thrilled to be painting something different. This was exactly what I set out to do. Practice my art and build a clientele. My life was perfect.

"It's not that far," I said. "Plus, I have a week off whenever I want but we should probably save that for the summer. And we have a long Fourth of July weekend." I kissed her softly. "I promise to give you every spare moment." I meant it. I knew we were still technically in the honeymoon phase of our relationship, but we genuinely had fun doing everything together.

"I know it's still cold, but how about a walk on the beach?" Olivia asked.

It was early April. The beach still had a winter feel to it, but I didn't care. "That sounds amazing. I've missed the beach."

We grabbed our jackets and scarves. It was sunny, but the wind coming off the water was cold. Even though we were wearing duck boots, we stayed away from the water and walked in the flat, hard sand where high tide had compacted it a few hours earlier. Olivia slipped her hand in mine and I pulled her closer. She looked happy and amazing. I was blessed with true love.

"Remember that time you were snooty to me?" I pointed to the dune where she used to sit almost every night.

She pinched my side. "You were flaunting yourself. You were like a bird fluffing your feathers to get my attention."

I laughed at the absurdity of her statement. "I barely got in your way."

"I'm glad you did." She smiled and it took my breath away. As much as we teased one another, we both knew how vulnerable we had to be in order to become us.

❖

"I can't tell you how happy I am to see you two together." Cassie squeezed my forearm with excitement after Olivia excused herself to go to the restroom. The four of us were having dinner at Remington's. The Wellingtons had returned to Revere Estates for the summer.

"It's been amazing. You both were right all along. I just needed to give her the space to adjust to another relationship," I said.

Brook smirked and shrugged. She didn't bother saying I told you so.

I laughed. "I know, I know. And it's because of both of you that we ended up here. Olivia is such a beautiful person." I was in love. Like the deepest kind of love. The kind that squeezed my heart every time I saw her or thought about her.

"Olivia seems like a new person and I love the change," Cassie said. She leaned closer. "It's because of you."

I felt like the grin on my face couldn't have been any larger. "I'm so fucking happy," I blurted out. They laughed.

"What's so funny?" Olivia asked. She slipped back into her seat and placed the linen napkin in her lap.

I took her hand. "I was telling our friends that I'm happy."

She arched her brow. "And that made you all laugh?"

I lowered my voice. "It was my word choice. I said I was so fucking happy and I meant it. Every single word."

She blushed and looked down at our hands. "I'm so fucking happy, too," she said.

Brook held up her wine glass. "We should toast this moment." We obliged and held our glasses so the rims touched. "Here's to another fantastic summer in Goda."

"Here's to love and another fantastic summer in Goda," Cassie said.

"Here's to finding love again and another fantastic summer in Goda," Olivia said.

They all looked at me expectantly. I thought for about two seconds. "Here's to true love, another fantastic summer in Goda, and making more memories I'll forever cherish."

About the Author

Multi-award-winning author Kris Bryant was born in Tacoma, WA, but has lived all over the world and now considers Kansas City her home. She received her B.A. in English from the University of Missouri and spends a lot of her time buried in books. She enjoys binge-watching TV, photography, kayaking, and spending time with her internet famous pooch, Molly.

Her first novel, *Jolt*, was a Lambda Literary Finalist. *Forget Me Not* was selected by the American Library Association's 2018 Over the Rainbow book list. *Breakthrough* won a 2019 Goldie for Contemporary Romance. *Listen* won a 2020 Goldie for Contemporary Romance. *Temptation* won a 2021 Goldie for Contemporary Romance. Written under the name Brit Ryder, *Not Guilty* won a 2022 Goldie for Erotic Romance. Kris can be reached at krisbryantbooks@gmail.com or www.krisbryant.net, @krisbryant14.

Books Available from Bold Strokes Books

An Independent Woman by Kit Meredith. Alex and Rebecca's attraction won't stop smoldering, despite their reluctance to act on it and incompatible poly relationship styles. (978-1-63679-553-9)

Cherish by Kris Bryant. Josie and Olivia cherish the time spent together, but when the summer ends and their temporary romance melts into the real deal, reality gets complicated. (978-1-63679-567-6)

Cold Case Heat by Mary P. Burns. Sydney Hansen receives a threat in a very cold murder case that sends her to the police for help where she finds more than justice with Detective Gale Sterling. (978-1-63679-374-0)

Proximity by Jordan Meadows. Joan really likes Ellie, but being alone with her could turn deadly unless she can keep her dangerous powers under control. (978-1-63679-476-1)

Sweet Spot by Kimberly Cooper Griffin. Pro surfer Shia Turning will have to take a chance if she wants to find the sweet spot. (978-1-63679-418-1)

The Haunting of Oak Springs by Crin Claxton. Ghosts and the past haunt the supernatural detective in a race to save the lesbians of Oak Springs farm. (978-1-63679-432-7)

Transitory by J.M. Redmann. The cops blow it off as a customer surprised by what was under the dress, but PI Micky Knight knows they're wrong—she either makes it her case or lets a murderer go free to kill again. (978-1-63679-251-4)

Unexpectedly Yours by Toni Logan. A private resort on a tropical island, a feisty old chief, and a kleptomaniac pet pig bring Suzanne and Allie together for unexpected love. (978-1-63679-160-9)

Bones of Boothbay Harbor by Michelle Larkin. Small-town police chief Frankie Stone and FBI Special Agent Eve Huxley must set aside their differences and combine their skills to find a killer after a burial site is discovered in Boothbay Harbor, Maine. (978-1-63679-267-5)

Crush by Ana Hartnett Reichardt. Josie Sanchez worked for years for the opportunity to create her own wine label, and nothing will stand in her way. Not even Mac, the owner's annoyingly beautiful niece Josie's forced to hire as her harvest intern. (978-1-63679-330-6)

Decadence by Ronica Black, Renee Roman, and Piper Jordan. You are cordially invited to Decadence, Las Vegas's most talked about invitation-only Masquerade Ball. Come for the entertainment and stay for the erotic indulgence. We guarantee it'll be a party that lives up to its name. (978-1-63679-361-0)

Gimmicks and Glamour by Lauren Melissa Ellzey. Ashly has learned to hide her Sight, but as she speeds toward high school graduation she must protect the classmates she claims to hate from an evil that no one else sees. (978-1-63679-401-3)

Heart of Stone by Sam Ledel. Princess Keeva Glantor meets Maeve, a gorgon forced to live alone thanks to a decades-old lie, and together the two women battle forces they formerly thought to be good in the hopes of leading lives they can finally call their own. (978-1-63679-407-5)

Murder at the Oasis by David S. Pederson. Palm trees, sunshine, and murder await Mason Adler and his friend Walter as they travel from Phoenix to Palm Springs for what was supposed to be a relaxing vacation but ends up being a trip of mystery and intrigue. (978-1-63679-416-7)

Peaches and Cream by Georgia Beers. Adley Purcell is living her dreams owning Get the Scoop ice cream shop until national dessert chain Sweet Heaven opens less than two blocks away and Adley has to compete with the far too heavenly Sabrina James. (978-1-63679-412-9)

The Only Fish in the Sea by Angie Williams. Will love overcome years of bitter rivalry for the daughters of two crab fishing families in this queer modern-day spin on Romeo and Juliet? (978-1-63679-444-0)

Wildflower by Cathleen Collins. When a plane crash leaves eleven-year-old Lily Andrews stranded in the vast wilderness of Arkansas, will she be able to overcome the odds and make it back to civilization and the one person who holds the key to her future? (978-1-63679-621-5)

Witch Finder by Sheri Lewis Wohl. Tamsin, the Keeper of the Book of Darkness, is in terrible danger, and as a Witch Finder, Morrigan must protect her and the secrets she guards even if it costs Morrigan her life. (978-1-63679-335-1)

A Second Chance at Life by Genevieve McCluer. Vampires Dinah and Rachel reconnect, but a string of vampire killings begin and evidence seems to be pointing at Dinah. They must prove her innocence while finding out if the two of them are still compatible after all these years. (978-1-63679-459-4)

Digging for Heaven by Jenna Jarvis. Litz lives for dragons. Kella lives to kill them. The last thing they expect is to find each other attractive. (978-1-63679-453-2)

Forever's Promise by Missouri Vaun. Wesley Holden migrated west disguised as a man for the hope of a better life and with no designs to take a wife, but Charlotte Rose has other ideas. (978-1-63679-221-7)

Here For You by D. Jackson Leigh. A horse trainer must make a difficult business decision that could save her father's ranch from foreclosure but destroy her chance to win the heart of a feisty barrel racer vying for a spot in the National Rodeo Finals. (978-1-63679-299-6)

I Do, I Don't by Joy Argento. Creator of the romance algorithm, Nicole Hart doesn't expect to be starring in her own reality TV dating show, and falling for the show's executive producer Annie Jackson could ruin everything. (978-1-63679-420-4)

It's All in the Details by Dena Blake. Makeup artist Lane Donnelly and wedding planner Helen Trent can't stand each other, but they must set aside their differences to ensure Darcy gets the wedding of her dreams, and make a few of their own dreams come true. (978-1-63679-430-3)

Marigold by Melissa Brayden. Marigold Lavender vows to take down Alexis Wakefield, the harsh food critic who blasts her younger sister's restaurant. If only she wasn't as sexy as she is mean. (978-1-63679-436-5)

The Town that Built Us by Jesse J. Thoma. When her father dies, Grace Cook returns to her hometown and tries to avoid Bonnie Whitlock, the woman who pulverized her heart, only to discover her father's estate has been left to them jointly. (978-1-63679-439-6)

A Degree to Die For by Karis Walsh. A murder at the University of Washington's Classics Department brings Professor Antigone Weston and Sergeant Adriana Kent together—first as opposing forces, and then allies as they fight together to protect their campus from a killer. (978-1-63679-365-8)

A Talent Within by Suzanne Lenoir. Evelyne, born into nobility, and Annika, a peasant girl with a deadly secret, struggle to change their destinies in Valmora, a medieval world controlled by religion, magic, and men. (978-1-63679-423-5)

Finders Keepers by Radclyffe. Roman Ashcroft's past, it seems, is not so easily forgotten when fate brings her and Tally Dewilde together—along with an attraction neither welcomes. (978-1-63679-428-0)

Homeland by Kristin Keppler and Allisa Bahney. Dani and Kate have finally found themselves on the same side of the war, but a new threat from the inside jeopardizes the future of the wasteland. (978-1-63679-405-1)

Just One Dance by Jenny Frame. Will Taylor Spark and her new business to make dating special—the Regency Romance Club—bring sparkle back to Jaq Bailey's lonely world? (978-1-63679-457-0)

On My Way There by Jaycie Morrison. As Max traverses the open road, her journey of impossible love, loss, and courage mirrors her voyage of self-discovery leading to the ultimate question: If she can't have the woman of her dreams, will the woman of real life be enough? (978-1-63679-392-4)

Transitioning Home by Heather K O'Malley. An injured soldier realizes they need to transition to really heal. (978-1-63679-424-2)

Truly Enough by JJ Hale. Chasing the spark of creativity may ignite a burning romance or send a friendship up in flames. (978-1-63679-442-6)

Vintage and Vogue by Kelly and Tana Fireside. When tech whiz Sena Abrigo marches into small-town Owen Station, she turns librarian Hazel Butler's life upside down in the most wonderful of ways, setting off an explosive series of events, threatening their chance at love…and their very lives. (978-1-63679-448-8)

9 781636 795676